A DEATH AT DINNER

A MARY BLAKE MYSTERY

A. G. BARNETT

ODDMOOR PRESS

MAILING LIST

CHAPTER ONE

Mary, Dot, and Pea were slumped on the wooden bench in the echoing corridor as they stared off into space with unseeing eyes. Mary's throat felt dry. If she could have spoken a word, she would have asked in a firm voice for a gin and tonic. Instead, she unfolded the small sheet of paper the auctioneer's assistant had handed her and stared at the number. There were a lot of zeros.

They had been ushered into a corridor at the back of the auction room, away from the baying press who had been stalking them since the discovery that had led them here.

"Did that just really happen?" Pea said from her right.

"It did," Dot replied from her left.

"Bloody hell," Pea added.

"That about sums it up." Mary nodded, finally finding her voice.

There was another period of silence until Mary stood up and rammed the piece of paper into the inside pocket of her tan leather jacket. "Right, I think it's high time we all went to the nearest pub to drink gin and tonic until all of this makes some sense."

There were dazed murmurs of agreement as the others rose from their seats and the three of them moved along the corridor towards the discreet rear entrance that an employee of the auction house had assured them would provide an escape from the press pack.

"Mary! Mary Blake!"

She turned to see a round, tubby man waddling down the corridor towards them.

"Mary, how do you feel about the record sale of the Fabergé egg you recently discovered?"

Mary frowned at him, wondering how the reporter had evaded security to find his way back here.

"Do you know?" she said, folding her arms. "I have absolutely no idea, but I'm sure I'll work it out in time."

The man stopped, frowning in confusion, as a security guard appeared behind him at a run and steered him back towards the public area with a firm clasp of his arm. Mary turned away and pushed open the doors before stepping into the bright sunlight.

"They will not leave you alone after this you know," Pea said, sighing as he followed her out and they headed down the road.

"Oh, they'll get bored, eventually. Now I'm not on TV, I'm nowhere near as much of a pull for them. This will do," she said, pointing down the street to a ramshackle pub.

Inside, the light was appropriately gloomy for a central London pub that had probably been serving pints to the city's citizens for hundreds of years. Mary and Dot took up residence at a well-worn and sticky table in the corner while Pea gathered them all gin and tonics at the bar.

"Well at least this means you've got the money to keep me employed," Dot said as she pulled a tissue and wiped the portion of the table in front of her.

"Quite the opposite," Mary said with a glint in her eye. "I need not work at all anymore, a personal assistant seems rather pointless, don't you think?"

"I think we both know that you don't pay me to help you professionally, you need me to make sure you can get through any twenty-four-hour period without descending into chaos."

"Point well made, if a little harshly," Mary answered as Pea arrived and placed their drinks before them. He sat heavily onto a battered wooden chair and sighed, his cheeks were flushed as red as his hair from the excitement and adrenaline of the auction, he looked tired.

The three of them seemed to have been at the centre of a whirlwind since they had discovered a Fabergé egg thought to have been lost for over a hundred years. Mary and Pea's grandfather had been entrusted the egg by a Russian man whose identity was unknown, their parents had later hidden it in the wall of a village graveyard. Now, brought back into the world from its hiding place by Mary, her brother Pea and her friend Dot, it had been identified as the Alexander III commemorative Fabergé egg, thought lost in the tumultuous fall of the Romanov's as Russia's ruling family. It had sold for twenty-one million dollars, and now they had to decide what they would do with it, and the rest of their lives.

"So what about you big brother?" Mary said, turning to him. "You don't have to worry about keeping the estate above water at least, but what next for it?"

"I don't want to run it at all anymore."

Mary blinked in surprise. "The estate?"

Pea looked up at her. "Of course, the estate! I'm finally free of it!"

"But I thought you enjoyed it?!"

"Oh, really Mary," Dot said with a tut and shake of her head. "For someone who professes to be such a people person, you do miss what's right under your nose sometimes."

Mary's gaze switched between her friend and her brother in confusion, causing Dot to roll her eyes.

"Mary," Pea said leaning forward, "I never wanted to run the estate, it was always dad's thing, not mine."

"Then why on earth did you do it?!"

Pea laughed. "Oh come on! You know it would have broken dad if I hadn't taken it on. It was all he ever wanted. He wanted the family to stay at Blancham forever, and that would only happen if we could somehow make the estate self-sustaining."

"And now you have the money..." Mary said, thinking the implications of this through.

"... I can hire a full-time estate manager," Pea continued, "and finally do something I want to do."

As he spoke, his eyes glazed over, his voice trailing off.

"So what's that going to be?" Dot asked.

"I have absolutely no idea," he said in a hollow voice.

"Well, that makes two of us," Mary said, lifting her glass to clink against his.

"Three actually," Dot said, raising hers.

"Do you know?" Mary said after a moment of silence, "There's a saying that I think is appropriate right about now." They both looked up at her expectantly. "They say that money can't buy you happiness, but I'd like to test the theory."

The others laughed and suddenly the tension of the morning cleared as though a storm had released an oppressive humidity.

Mary's phone buzzed in her jeans' pocket. She pulled it out and glanced at the number calling, unrecognised.

"Hello?" she said, placing the device to her ear.

"Mary? It's Spencer, Spencer Harley."

Her brow wrinkled as she tried to place the name. "Spencer Harley?" she said, looking at Pea carefully to gauge his reaction.

"Spencer from that holiday in France?" Pea said in a whisper, "With mum and dad?"

"Yes," Spencer continued, "I know it's been a while, but I wondered if I could invite you down to my neck of the woods for the weekend?"

"Oh, right," Mary said, unsure of what to say.

"There's a restaurant down here that's having an anniversary bash and thought you might want to join us?"

"Right, well that sounds nice, but..."

"I've seen you in the papers recently and I think it would be of some interest to you…"

Mary paused. She had been in the papers recently. Being credited with catching the murderer of a young actress who was your arch-rival, tended to do that. Especially when soon after you discover a missing treasure of the art world.

"Could you just hold on a moment?" she said before covering the mouthpiece.

"It's Spencer Harley, he wants me to go to some restaurant bash this weekend, something to do with me being in the paper."

"Say yes," Dot said immediately. They both turned to her. "We've all just being saying that we need to figure out what we do next," she said, "maybe we don't need to figure it out, maybe we just need to go with the flow and see where it takes us. Ask if we can all come, I could do with a nice meal."

Mary's mouth fell open at this unusually carefree attitude of her oldest friend, but she didn't have time to be suspicious, Spencer was still on the phone.

"Yes Spencer, that would be lovely," she answered, eyeing Dot carefully. "Would it be ok if my brother and friend came along as well?"

"Of course! The more the merrier! Let me give you the details."

CHAPTER TWO

"I'm sure you're just being paranoid," Pea said, his mouth half full of an egg mayonnaise sandwich freshly procured from the train's buffet car.

Mary had spent the last ten minutes explaining that, now they were on the train to the small town where the rather mysterious invitation had come from, she had a bad feeling about the whole thing. Her recent exposure had made her feel uncomfortable, but not in the way she had expected. After playing the role of a female detective on television for so long, she had found it strangely thrilling to be part of solving a case in the real world. The feeling of pride and exhilaration though had been tempered when she remembered that, no matter what she had thought of the victim, a young life had been lost.

"I mean," Pea continued, "if he's something to do with this restaurant and wants some publicity, who better to call than you right now? You're all over the papers and let's face it, being involved in solving a murder and then finding a lost artefact is pretty hot stuff where the press is concerned. I bet whoever is publicising this bash couldn't believe their luck when he said he knew you!"

"He doesn't know me though, does he?" Mary countered from the seat opposite him. "We met on a family holiday, god knows how many years ago, and that was it!"

"Maybe he wants you to solve a crime," Dot said with a mocking, malevolent tone.

"Don't be mean Dot, it doesn't suit you."

The truth was, the thought had occurred to Mary as well. There had been something in Spencer's tone. His voice had been too light and airy, as though he was intent on making the call seem as though it was nothing out of the ordinary. It was anything but. Calling something after one meeting all that time ago. It was strange, to say the least. Also, the publicity Mary had recently received could hardly be ignored, and he had mentioned the papers.

After she had played a part in solving the murder of Melanie Shaw, her brother's housekeeper and cook had then spoken to the papers. Unfortunately, beloved Hetty had a tendency to exaggerate and the resulting articles and headlines had made her sound like a mixture of Sherlock Holmes and Wonder Woman, telling the press that she had solved the case single-handedly and saving an incompetent police force in the process. This, of all things, had worried Mary the most. As much as she hated to admit it, Inspector Joe Corrigan, who had worked the case, had affected her. It made the back of her neck prickle with heat every time she thought of him reading those newspaper articles and cursing her for taking the limelight and making him look a fool. It bothered her in a way she couldn't quite put her finger on.

"Don't you think it's odd that he's paying for us to stay in a hotel in Parchester?" Mary said, trying to distract herself from her thoughts. "I mean, if he's been reading the papers he knows that we're not exactly short of a bob or two."

"He isn't either from what I've heard," Pea said, "he's got some huge estate just outside Parchester and puts on all kinds of food festivals, classic car shows and things. I was looking at trying to emulate some of his ideas for Blancham, actually." Mary glanced at him as he chuckled to himself. "I guess that will be someone else's job now."

"Have you started advertising for the position of estate manager yet?" Dot chipped in from the back seat.

"No,"

"I can help if you'd like? I might as well be your PA if Mary can't make any use of me."

"You just hold your horses, Dot Tanner," Mary said, "if you're forcing me to still pay you even though I don't need your services, I think I should decide if you can work for my brother."

"Oh come on Mary," Pea said, shooting her the glance of a disappointed sibling.

"Oh fine," Mary said with a sigh. "Don't worry about me, you two just go ahead and make your arrangements."

"Will do," said Dot with a satisfied smile.

Two hours later and the train was shuddering into the quaint station at Parchester. With only two platforms and one small, low slung building painted bright blue, the scene felt more to Mary as though it was a TV set rather than a real functioning transport hub. For a moment, her mind harked back to her many years playing Susan Law on the hit show Her Law and she gave a slight shudder. Those days were gone, and she still wasn't used to it.

"Now we're rich," Mary said as she heaved her

case off the train, "shouldn't we have people to do this?"

"If you hire people to do everything for you, then you're not really living," Dot said, pulling her case down.

Mary paused and looked at her. Sometimes she had the impression that Dot was secretly very philosophical, which to Mary, as a woman who lived more 'in the moment' and tended towards action rather than deep reflection, seemed like something strange and curious to be observed. The moments from Dot were fleeting though, and only appeared in between her usual demeanour of rigidly practical, more 'just getting on with it'.

They passed through the turnstile which was left open and unmanned, rendering their tickets pointless, and moved through the small building to the doors which led out onto the street. The station seemed to be situated quite centrally in the small town, and the road they found themselves on buzzed with activity. Cars trundled back and forth in front of them along the narrow street, and on the far side people milled about a row of shops that looked as though they had stood there for decades. Small, but pretty Christmas decorations criss-crossed down the street, and although not lit in the day, Mary sensed they would be lovely at night. Mary couldn't help but feel the warm, festive atmosphere of the town despite the cold.

"So, where do you think we'd find a taxi?" Pea said looking up and down the road.

"No need," Mary said, pointing. At the end of the street to their right stood a grand Victorian building with large gold lettering adorning its side, which declared it to be the Rudolph Hotel.

Although the bright sunshine and pale blue sky had lured people from their homes and places of work on this Friday afternoon, there was no avoiding the fact that it was bitterly cold. People were wrapped up against the icy gusts that whipped around the small street with scarves pulled up over their mouths and bobble hats pulled down low. Mary was regretting her decision to wear a skirt, even if she did have thick tights on below. They hurried along without speaking until they stepped into the warm and inviting lobby of the hotel with a sigh of relief.

"Mary!" a voice bellowed at them before they'd even come to a stop. A heavily jowled man with a rotund figure bounded towards them, his arms open wide. "Delighted to see you!" he added as he air-kissed Mary's cheeks.

"Oh, hello Spencer," Mary managed, somewhat bewildered. "I hadn't realised you were going to meet us."

"Well of course! Couldn't have my guests of honour not greeted, eh? Percy, good to see you," he said, shaking Pea by the hand.

"And you, Spencer, it's been too long. This is our friend Dot Tanner."

"Delighted to meet you!" Spencer bowed. Despite his large frame, he was full of such nervous energy that he seemed to be moving even when he was stood still. "Now, I've made all the arrangements. All you need to do is grab your room keys and get settled in. I thought we could maybe meet for drinks in, say, an hour? I wondered though Mary if I could have a quick word with you alone before you go up?"

"Oh, yes of course." She nodded to the others in response to their questioning looks and watched them make their way to the large reception desk. Spencer guided her across the large wood-panelled lobby to a seating area where they both sat in leather-bound wingback chairs.

"Now Mary, I realise you must be wondering why I invited you here all of a sudden."

"It had crossed my mind yes."

He smiled nervously and then looked around as though checking no one else was in earshot. "I don't like beating about the bush," he continued in a low voice, "much rather get it out in the open and get on with it."

"Right…" Mary said slowly, wondering where on earth this was going.

"The thing is," he looked around again, "it seems I'm being blackmailed."

"Blackmailed?!"

"Shh!" he cried, waving his hands at her in a panic as his eyes darted around the large room. "Please, be discreet!"

"I'm sorry," Mary continued in a whisper, leaning forward in her chair, "But you took me by surprise there. What do you mean blackmailed?"

"I mean what I say! Someone's been sending me threatening notes, I received another one just this morning!"

"What are they threatening you with?"

His face flushed a deeper crimson than it already was. "I couldn't tell you," he said rather gruffly, "They claim to know some secret about me, but that's not important, what is important is finding out who's sending them."

"Well, have you gone to the police?"

"Good lord, no! In this town, that would be as good as advertising it to the world! I love the place, but it is home to the most terrible gossips."

Now that the initial surprise was wearing off,

Mary had a sudden sinking feeling that she knew where this was headed.

"And why does this have anything to do with me?" she asked, already knowing the answer.

"Well, I saw what you did with that murder recently and I thought you might be just the person to help me out, you know, do a little investigating. After all, an old family friend and all that, easy for you to hang around the place for a while and see what you can make of it, eh?"

Mary opened her mouth to say that the man was an idiot. That he should stop worrying about his reputation and go straight to the police rather than putting his faith in an actress who had merely played the role of a detective rather than being one. Instead, though, she realised with a jolt that the feeling that had been growing in the pit of her stomach from the moment Spencer has said the word blackmail, wasn't one of fear or worry, it was one of excitement. When she did finally speak, she surprised herself.

"I will do my best to help, but you'll need to show me the notes and tell me everything you know and let me know of anyone you suspect."

"Right," Spencer said, blinking. "Well, now that that's out of the way, I'll let you get settled." He rose from his chair and gestured with his hand towards the reception desk. "I'll see you and your friends at the bar in an hour, shall I?"

"Of course," Mary said, trying not to show her disappointment that she wasn't going to find out more right there and then. She moved away towards the desk with her mind racing.

CHAPTER THREE

"Blackmail?" Pea said, his mouth gaping.

"That's what he said," Mary answered as she pushed in her earrings. "He invited me here to look into it."

"Who does he think we are?" Dot asked in an incredulous tone, "the Scooby-Doo gang or something?!"

"Look," Mary said, turning to them. "I told him he should go to the police, but he said he doesn't want to because the whole town is full of gossips. So if he's not going to go to the authorities, there's no harm in us having a look, is there?" The two of them looked back at her with somewhat conflicted expressions. "Oh, come on you two! Have you forgotten how much fun we had when we were running around trying to catch a murderer?! And then when we followed the clues to find the egg and look how that turned out!"

"It was the most fun I've had in years." Pea grinned. They both turned to Dot, who sighed and shook her head.

"You two are going to be the death of me."

"So that's settled then!" Mary said as she sprayed herself with perfume, "We'll help Spencer look into this blackmail business and see if we can assist."

"As long as you promise that if anything seems to be getting serious, we call the police," Dot said firmly.

"Yes Mother," Mary answered rolling her eyes. "So, are you two ready?"

"Well, you only gave us ten minutes before barging into our rooms and dragging us to yours, but yes, I'll do," Dot said, smoothing her cardigan down.

"Come on then, let's find out what all this is about!" Mary said, bouncing towards the doorway.

The hotel had an old-world quality to it, but without feeling too dated. Many years ago, the place had been given the kind of rich and opulent decor that didn't need modernising or updating. Yes, it was a little faded around the edges, but that only seemed to add to the feeling of longstanding quality from a bygone age. The rooms were large and furnished with solid mahogany furniture. The vast central atrium and lobby contained a wide wooden staircase which wound its way up either wall to the five floors above. Mary felt, as she descended, that they could have been in some old Hollywood movie from the twenties where a glamorous actress would undoubtedly find love with some strong and brooding lead. For a brief moment, she found her thoughts drifting to Inspector Joe Corrigan. She had heard nothing from him in the last month or so since their paths had crossed on a murder case, yet something about him lingered in her mind like an itch that needed scratching.

They moved through the lobby and through an archway that led to a comfortable looking room. Leather sofas were mixed with more standard table and chairs, again everything had the aged look of quality. Spencer Harley leaned against the dark wood of the bar and raised his glass to the party.

"So then, what can I get you all?"

"Gin and tonic for me," Mary said moving towards him, "and I guess these two will have the same?" The others nodded their agreement and Spencer ordered from a young barman with a moustache and goatee arrangement that made him look as though he was a budding amateur magician.

He also sported a fresh and very sore looking black eye. "Right," Mary said, determined to get down to business as soon as possible. "I've filled my gang in, so let's talk about these letters shall we?"

Spencer's face paled as he looked up sharply at the barman. "Why don't we go and find a table? Er, James? Could you bring our drinks over when they're ready? There's a good chap."

The young man nodded silently and continued with his task as Spencer hurried away. They followed him to a quiet corner where two leather sofas faced each other.

"I'd be grateful if you could be more discreet," he said, his face ruddy.

"I'm sorry," Mary said, looking over her shoulder at the barman on the other side of the room. "So you suspect the barman?"

"James? Oh, I don't know about that. I would just like to keep this between us," he looked at Pea and Dot, "though I see that's already not possible."

"Oh Dot and Pea are OK," Mary said dismissively. "Souls of discretion, the both of them. Besides, we come as a team, so if you want our help we'll need to know everything."

The barman, James, appeared with a tray of drinks and they fell silent, only muttering thanks until he had left.

"So come on," Mary said eagerly, turning to Spencer who was sitting next to her on the sofa and taking a large swig of what she had to admit was excellently mixed gin and tonic, "let us have it."

Spencer looked nervously between them all and cleared his throat. "Well, it all started a couple of months ago when a note was pushed under my door here at the hotel."

"You were staying here?" Mary asked.

"Oh, I have a permanent room. A perk of being part owner."

"So I'm guessing you stay here at the hotel a lot?"

Spencer frowned, "What on earth has that got to do with anything?"

"If someone knows enough about you to blackmail you, then they probably know enough to know where you live, it's not far from here is it?"

"No, just a few miles outside of town," Spencer stuttered, looking pale. He took a large swig of the whiskey that stood before him on the table.

"So someone knew that you were at your hotel room quite a bit and would find the note," Mary continued thoughtfully. "Do housekeeping have access to your room?"

"No," Spencer shook his head, making his double chin wobbly vigorously. "My room is more like a personal flat of mine, quite separate from the hotel. I do allow Daisy in once a week to do a good clean though."

"Daisy?" Pea asked.

"Daisy White, she organises our cleaning staff who are from an external company, she does other things around the place too. The girl is a godsend." He took another large gulp of whiskey and sighed. "To tell you the truth," he said leaning forward, "the hotel doesn't make a great deal of money other than the restaurant and we have to have a bit of a skeleton staff. The tourist trade for Parchester isn't what it used to be, I'm afraid, especially in winter."

"Ok," Mary said, "back to the note, what did it say?"

"Oh nothing in particular," Spencer said with a dismissive hand gesture. "Just how they knew what I was up to and all that business. Said that they wanted money."

"And did they say where you had to send the money? Or leave it somewhere?"

He frowned again, his head tilting on one side as though deciding something. "No, I don't think any of them did. Just said they wanted money."

"Any of them?" Dot said. "How many have you had?"

"Oh, I think I'm up to four now," he sighed again, leaning back in his chair.

"And are you sure there's nothing you can think of that gives them cause to think you could be blackmailed?" Mary asked gently. "I mean, they did say they knew what you were up to. What could that relate to?"

"No, of course not, not a clue what it's all about. Don't worry about all that, just find out who's sending them." Spencer bridled, but the reddening of his cheeks made Mary think otherwise. She glanced at the others and saw that they were thinking the same. She decided not to push it, for now, maybe they would know more when they saw the notes.

"So, tell me about your situation," Mary continued, "do you live with anyone?"

"No, I live alone."

"And where you live, does anyone else have access to it?"

"I have a cleaning company come once a week, they have a key."

Mary turned to ask if someone could take notes but saw that Dot had already pulled a notepad from her handbag and dutifully jotting things down.

"We'll need the name of the cleaning company, you could have left some confidential papers lying around that someone there saw."

"Oh no, it's nothing like that, I'm sure. I don't

keep anything of note outside of my wall safe and no one sees inside there but me."

"So the hotel then," Mary continued, "you say you're a part-owner, who is your partner?"

"That would be Roderick Sutton," Spencer said coldly. "Truth be told I wish I'd never got into business with the fellow, but we are where we are."

"Why do you regret it?" Pea asked. "Is the chap not pulling his weight?"

"Oh, neither of us does much if I'm being honest. We have a hotel manager who takes care of everything, Edward Landry, his name is. No, it's just Roderick is one of those go-get-em types, young and ambitious. Persuaded me to go in on this place with him when I didn't care a jot for the hotel business! Still, he does fuss so, always looking to change things. It's enough to tire one out just talking with him."

"This Edward Landry, what's he like?"

"Oh, he's a fish-faced bore of a man but good at keeping things running smoothly, I have to give him that. Lord knows how he does it. I try to stay out of the whole business. We don't have much in the way of staff really, we have a couple of young lads from the town we call in if we get busy, which between you and me isn't very often these days, but other than that it's mostly all about the restaurant."

"And who works there?" Pea asked.

"Well, there's Anna of course," he looked at their blank expressions for a moment before continuing. "Anna Crosby? You haven't heard of her?"

"Afraid not." Mary shrugged apologetically.

"Well she's been making quite a name for herself at the restaurant here, we received a Michelin star just two months ago you know."

"Congratulations. So I take it this Anna woman is the head chef?"

"That's right, wonderful she is. Then there's Thomas Mosley and Ruth Faulkner who both work with her, all very talented. I must say it's all come together very nicely, despite all the problems. We hope that it will lead to things with the hotel itself picking up."

"Problems?"

"Oh, you know, the normal issues when you're trying to start something up. Refrigerator breaks down, a pipe starts leaking. All costs money and time, but we got through it.

Mary took another sip of her gin and tonic and leaned back against the soft leather of the sofa. This didn't seem to be getting them anywhere. Spencer was being so vague over the blackmail letters that she had the impression he was either lying or genuinely had no idea what he was being threatened with. Either way, his seemingly quiet life lived between his country home and the hotel didn't seem much cause for intrigue. She was going to have to do some digging without Spencer. If he wasn't willing to be completely straight with her, maybe the people who knew him would be.

"Of course," Spencer continued, "you'll get to meet everyone tonight at the rehearsal."

"Rehearsal? Rehearsal for what?"

He looked at her in mild surprise. "Why of course, that's the reason you're here as far as anybody else knows."

Mary, Dot and Pea exchanged blank looks.

"Didn't I tell you? Oh, well, tomorrow night is our special Christmas fundraiser for the local hospice. You know the kind of thing, dignitaries from the town, charity auction and all of that business. Of course, there will be a special meal prepared for the occasion and all the proceeds going to the worthy cause. Tonight we're having a little rehearsal meal for the staff as a kind of end-of-year bash. You're all welcome tonight of course, but tomorrow, you Mary, will be the guest of honour!"

"Oh," Mary said with a sense of dread. "How lovely." Her agent Tony had been forever sending her to far-flung corners of the United Kingdom to attend some charity function or a grand opening of a local landmark. She had endured for several years until the small, sweaty mayor of a town in Yorkshire, after boring her to death on his town's plan for a new car park, had pinched her bottom. She had sworn off such events ever since.

CHAPTER FOUR

They had left Spencer in the bar of the hotel and ventured out for lunch. Pea had gone his maximum period of roughly two hours since his last meal and was already getting tetchy. The hotel restaurant was not yet open and Spencer had been unhelpful when asked for recommendations so they had wandered down the pretty rows of shops that lined Parchester's main thoroughfare until they had seen a small café named 'The Tumbledown' and dived inside, deciding that it was cold enough outside to not be picky.

The cafe was small, but neat, with little round metal tables and chairs that were more suited to a patio than inside. They had, though, been covered with brightly coloured cushions and the bright spotlights and pictures that lined the walls showing different scenes and people of the town made it feel cosy and inviting.

"Oh!" a woman with a round face and welcoming eyes exclaimed as they approached the counter, her hands rising to her cheeks. "If it isn't Mary Blake in my café!"

"Hi," Mary said with a slight sense of dread, feeling the other people in the café turning to look at them.

"Oh, I just loved 'Her Law'," the woman gushed. "You were just brilliant in it!"

"Thank you," Mary smiled. "We were just looking to grab something to go for lunch," she said, hoping to move the conversation on and get out of here as soon as possible.

"Oh nonsense," the woman said with a wave of her hand. "You look bloody frozen from being outside, sit down and I'll bring you all a nice cup of tea."

"Thank you, but I'm not sure..."

"Oh don't worry, I'll make sure no one bothers you," the woman said grabbing three menus and gesturing at them to follow her.

Twenty minutes later the three of them were each tucking into a toasted panini and listening to a brief history of Parchester from the café's owner who had introduced herself as Sandra. After listening politely while eating, Mary dabbed at her mouth with a serviette and decided to see what the town's apparently considerable grapevine had to say about the hotel.

"Oh that old place has been going downhill for years," Sandra said dismissively. "It was built when there was a railway line all the way to Tanbury from here, but when that closed down Parchester never got the visitors to keep a place like that running."

"What about the new owners? It was bought a couple of years ago, wasn't it?"

"Spencer Harley," Sandra nodded knowingly. "Bit of a figure around here, always putting things on at Sundown Manor and he's very generous with the town. Lovely man he is."

"And Roderick Sutton?" Dot asked.

"Well," Sandra said, her eyebrows raising, "he's a bit of a slippery one. Fancies himself a bit of a big-shot. I'll never understand why Mr Harley went in with him. Mr Harley is a cut above that kind of company, an honest to goodness gent."

Mary smiled and did her best to listen, but Sandra was off again on the past and future of the town she clearly loved and they soon made their excuses and left.

CHAPTER FIVE

Mary leaned on the railing of the Juliet balcony of her room and watched the buzz of the street below. An old man was walking an even older looking dog, a young mother hurried along with two children in front of her and a middle-aged couple stood, hand in hand, looking in the window of an estate agents. Mary sighed. All her life, the opposite sex had been something more akin to a hobby for her. She had had her share of playful dalliances, tempestuous relationships and downright lust-driven indulgences, but never anything serious. Never anything that had meant something to her in the way she had always thought it should have. The character she had played for so many years, Susan Law, had never had a long-term relationship either. The love interest for the fictional detective changing each season in order to keep the viewer entertained and to keep things 'fresh'. Was that what Mary was doing? Maybe she saw settling down as something to be feared, something that would rob her of her own identity? But what was her identity now? With her acting career over and enough money in the bank to forge a new path, what was it she wanted from life?

She sighed as she picked at the peeling paint of the railing. The only thing that had managed to set her pulse racing in years was being involved in solving the recent murder. That is of course, unless you include Detective Inspector Joe Corrigan. She had met him on the previous case, and he had immediately gotten under her skin. At first, annoying her, and then somehow charming her in a way she couldn't quite define. She felt her cheeks flush for a moment as she suddenly wondered whether she was involving herself in the investigation of another crime in order to raise the chances of seeing him again.

There was a knock at the door, making her shake herself back into the here and now as she headed across her room to answer it.

"Miss Blake, my name is Edward Landry and I'm the hotel manager here," said the man who stood framed in the doorway, "I don't want to disturb you, but just wanted to let you know how welcome you are and how much we appreciate you attending tomorrow's charity event."

Spencer's description of Landry flashed through her mind. Fish-faced was a decent phrase for him. He had a thin, pinched look but with puffy, pursed lips that seemed to be permanently pouting smugly even as he spoke. He wore a black suit with waistcoat and a white carnation in his buttonhole. Mary couldn't help but feel he was slightly overdressed against the shabby nature of the hotel decor behind him.

"It's nice to meet you Edward, would like to come in?"

His eyes widened momentarily in surprise before his resting face of fishy smugness returned.

"I would be delighted, but I mustn't stay too long. I have a lot to prepare for tomorrow."

"Of course," Mary said, stepping aside and letting him into the room.

He stood stiffly, awkwardly. Mary wondered if being in a guest's room was a more unusual experience for him than she would have thought.

"So, Edward, how long have you worked at the hotel?"

"Three years now, we're gradually getting it back on its feet."

"So it had been in trouble whcn you took over?"

"Well, I don't like to speak ill of the previous owners," he said in a manner that led Mary to believe there was actually nothing he enjoyed more, "but I would say they had let things slide somewhat. We've managed to rebuild our reputation though, gradually."

"That's fantastic, and I hear the restaurant has helped in that?"

His nostrils flared as his overall expression was one of someone who had just smelled something particularly pungent and unpleasant.

"The restaurant has done very well," he said in a somewhat forced voice, "but the hotel has been making excellent progress as well. It's been lovely talking to you, Miss Blake."

"Mary, please."

"Mary," a smile flickered onto his lips and then vanished again, "but I really must be going. I look forward to seeing you later."

"Yes, me too," Mary said, closing the door behind him.

She paused with her hand clasping the doorknob in thought. So, Edward Landry wasn't a fan of the restaurant? Why would that be? She wondered. Was it just that it was stealing the praise for getting the hotel back on its feet? Or was there something more to it than that?

CHAPTER SIX

"It could just be that he doesn't like the woman who runs it," Pea said as they descended the wide staircase towards the lobby. "Anna was her name, I think?"

"Anna Crosby," Dot replied. "I looked her up while I was waiting for Mary to get ready." There was an unmistakable undertone to her voice which made it quite clear that she had endured many years of waiting for Mary to 'get ready' for things. Mary ignored it.

"Well? What did you find?"

"She's definitely got a good reputation. Loads of articles in the local press saying what a talent she is, and now with this Michelin star, there's the talk of her on bigger sites online. Looks like she's making a name for herself in any case."

"Right," Mary said, pausing as they reached the bottom step and looking around the quiet lobby area. "We need to try to get as much information on everyone as we can. Until we see the letters and Spencer starts telling us everything, we're not going to be able to pin down who's blackmailing him. It might not even be anyone from here, but it's a place to start. The more we can work out about his life and the people in it, the more likely we stumble across something. OK?"

"Yes, sir!" Pea barked, pulling off a military salute and standing to attention.

"Oh, very funny," Mary said rolling her eyes and punching him lightly on the arm before heading towards the bar.

Pea grinned as he rubbed his arm and followed Mary with Dot. "Well, I have to admit, this is more fun than looking after the wretched estate."

"Yeah, well, let's hope it stays fun," Dot replied darkly.

"Something bothering you, Dot?" Pea said, his expressive face etched in concern.

"I know Mary likes to play these games, and it looks like you've caught the bug too. Even I got carried away with the idea when I first heard about it. We all just need to remember this could be serious. It could be dangerous. There's a reason the police handle things like this you know."

"Oh, it will be alright!" Pea said putting his arm around her. "As soon as we find anything real out we can hand it over to the plod. I don't intend facing up to anyone myself, I'm not built for the old fisticuffs!" As if to prove his point, he jabbed at an imaginary foe with his free left hand. Dot said nothing, but blushed quietly at the warmth of his arm around her shoulders.

The hotel bar was as quiet as it had been earlier in the day when they had visited. Spencer was leaning against the same spot as then and Mary wondered if he had actually left in the hours in-between at all. He was surrounded by a small group, all brandishing champagne flutes and chatting amongst themselves. This included the black-eyed barman who was bent over the bar to join the conversation.

"Mary!" Spencer called when the blonde woman had finished speaking and he had looked up and caught sight of her. "Come on over!"

The three of them moved over to the group and were introduced.

There were three women in the group. The most arresting of these was the person currently holding the attention of the others. She talked in an animated and excitable way, her hands gesticulating wildly to illustrate each point. She had tied-back blonde hair, bright wide eyes and an infectious personality that made Mary like her as soon as she saw her. As Spencer guided them over, the woman jumped forward excitedly to tell Mary what a fan she was, taking her hand in an enthusiastic grip and introducing herself as Ruth Faulkner who worked in the hotel restaurant. She was beautiful and full of the kind of vitality people in their mid-twenties have. Something that now Mary could only look back on in envy.

They were then introduced to Anna Crosby. Around Mary's age, she had a wide mouth and a high forehead topped by dark hair tied back in a ponytail. She seemed quiet, shy, and quite unlike Mary's image of a head chef which, admittedly, was mostly gained from reality television. She had expected her to be a surly and aggressive figure, not the rather meek woman before her.

The final woman was Daisy White. A young woman who had a round and pleasant face with small features that made her look even younger than she was. She said a self-conscious hello and bobbed a little in a half curtsey. Spencer had mentioned that she was responsible for many of the various jobs around the hotel, but Mary hadn't expected her to have quite such an air of old-world parlour maid, though she matched the hotel decor well.

Spencer then moved the introductions on to the men.

One was a very good-looking young man, all stubble jaw and lean muscles under his kitchen whites named Thomas Moseley, another kitchen employee. Then there was a man around mid-thirties with a beak-like nose and a quiff of brown hair. He wore a much more expensive suit than the one donned by the hotel manager, Edward Landry, who stood next to him looking like a cheap knock-off. This was Roderick Sutton, Spencer's partner in the hotel. He gave them each a firm handshake with strong eye contact and a charming smile.

"It really is so nice of you to come, it means a lot," he said as he reached Mary. "Parchester doesn't get a lot in the way of celebrities and I'm sure your presence will cause a stir in the town."

"Oh, I doubt anyone will be making a fuss over me anymore," Mary said, hoping to come across as modest rather than pathetic.

"Well, I for one can't wait to hear all your stories from the set of Her Law and in particular your recent escapades as a real-life detective!"

"I'm definitely sure no one wants to hear about that," she said dismissively as she turned towards

Anna Crosby. "Why don't we talk about this fabulous restaurant of yours instead? I believe congratulations are in order, you were recently awarded a Michelin star, I believe?"

"Oh, yes, that's right," stammered Anna, pushing her long dark hair behind her ears.

"Fully deserved," Thomas said from her right, the young man's voice sounding with a curiously flat tone. Anna looked up at him quickly, and then looked away again.

"Well, it's really a team effort," she said in her high pitch nervous voice.

"And what can we look forward to on tonight's menu?" Pea asked, grinning as he took glasses of champagne from James the barman and handed them to Mary and Dot.

"Oh, it's a surprise actually," Anna said.

Thomas gave a small snort and moved behind her to the bar.

"Oh, Anna won't care as long as there's wine with it, eh Anna?"

"We'd better be getting back soon hadn't we, Anna?" Ruth said suddenly, rather more loudly than was necessary in Mary's opinion.

"Oh, right. Yes," Anna replied. "Better get on." Anna moved towards the door as Ruth moved to Thomas and whispered something in his ear.

"I'll be there in a minute," he said quietly in response. Mary noticed a worried look on Ruth's face as she passed to follow her boss out of the room.

Spencer and Roderick had started up their own conversation and Edward had moved behind the bar in order to talk to James about something or other, so Mary turned her attention to Daisy.

"So, Daisy, how long have been working here at the hotel?"

"Oh, a long time!" she answered enthusiastically. "I started straight out of school. My dad used to work here before he retired."

"Ah, so a family tradition!"

The young girl beamed back. Mary guessed her age at around nineteen, but her rounded, plain face could well be making her look younger than she was.

"Now is not the time!" The group turned as one towards Spencer, whose voice had risen so suddenly.

"Alright, Spencer old chap," Roderick said, looking at the others with a small smile. "Let's talk about it later, shall we?"

Spencer gave a snort of derision and turned away from his partner and back to the group.

"Shall I get everyone another round of drinks?" Pea said, breaking the tense silence that had followed this exchange.

There was a murmur of agreement and Dot and

Pea made their way to the bar and began talking with the barman and Roderick while Spencer joined Mary and Daisy.

"Sorry about that," Spencer said gruffly. "Damn fellow never switches off from business for a second."

"Was there some sort of disagreement?" Mary asked innocently.

"Oh, no. All fine," Spencer blustered. "Now Daisy, have you been explaining to Mary what a little godsend you are to this place? Because you should have been!"

Daisy gave a coquettish half-smile and her cheeks coloured slightly. "I just do my job, Mr Harley."

"Now now, you know I've told you to call me Spencer, and in any case, I'd say it's more like you do four jobs nevermind one!"

Daisy gave a nervous laugh.

"So, come on then," Mary said smiling, "what do you do around here?"

"Oh, well, I organise the cleaners," she began, as though reading a mental list in her head. "They come from a company in town and I just make sure they're doing the right bits. Then I'm on reception most of the time, making sure I take the bookings that come in by phone, though most are online these days. And I make sure the rooms are all ready and I get in Andy the odd-job man from town to do bits and..." she looked up looking embarrassed. "Oh I'm sorry, I can go on a bit!"

"Don't be silly!" Mary laughed, "It's nice to see someone enjoying their job."

"Absolutely," Spencer bellowed. "And the hotel is lucky to have you!"

"I just hope we can restore it to what it was," she said in a shaky voice. "That's what my dad would have wanted."

Spencer cleared his throat and awkwardly patted her on the shoulder. "Yes, well. We'll all do our best, eh?"

She nodded and wiped her eyes on her sleeve. "Excuse me a minute, I just need to go and check on something."

Mary watched her go with a tinge of sadness.

"Poor thing," Spencer said hoarsely. "Her mother died years ago and her father was all she had left in the world really, well him and this place."

"And he died recently?"

"Just a couple of months ago. Heart attack, poor fellow. The chap had worked here for years. Did odd jobs around the place, even used to go hunting in Parchester Woods for the restaurant!" Spencer said, shaking his head and sighing at the memory of a man he clearly had admired.

"Well," Dot said arriving back with a tray of gin and tonics, "that Roderick is quite a one, isn't he?"

"Yes," Spencer said darkly, "isn't he?"

"What were you talking about?" Mary asked as she took one of the glasses, exchanging it for her now-empty champagne flute.

"Some new business venture he's part of, property development or something."

Spencer coughed suddenly. "Why don't you all go on through to the restaurant? I'm sure they're almost ready for us now." He moved across to the bar where he began talking to James, the barman.

"Right," Roderick said, appearing with Pea at his side. "Follow us, ladies!" They moved out into the lobby and towards a door at the back of the room, which led down into a short passage.

"Obviously the restaurant has a main entrance onto the street as well," he said as they made their way down the corridor, "the space isn't much to write home about, but the food is bloody good. I have to give that to Anna."

Something in his tone played at the back of Mary's mind, but she soon dismissed it as they stepped out into the restaurant.

She wasn't sure what she had been expecting, but it definitely wasn't this. In contrast to the shabby, old-world charm of the hotel, the restaurant was trendy to the point of overdoing it. Industrial looking lamps hung low over the immaculately laid tables, each placed a discreet distance from each other. The walls were exposed brick and upper pipework while the floor was polished concrete. The overall feel was one more of a high-end central London restaurant than hotel eatery in a provincial town.

"We're here I think," Roderick said, pointing to a large table that had been set out in the middle of the room. "I just have some calls to make, but I'll join you soon." He flashed a smile at them all and then vanished back the way they had come.

"Blimey, this is all a bit strange, isn't it?" Mary said as they took their seats/ "Where is everyone?" She looked around the empty restaurant.

"Oh they've closed it for the evening for us," Pea said as he began tearing at a seeded roll from one of the baskets on the table. "James told me, he's closing the bar up as well in a bit. There are only three guests staying here at the moment and they're all passing through on business and have been told the place is basically shutting down tonight."

"Well, you've been busy," Mary said, impressed.

"You're not the only one who can play sleuth in the family, you know!" he said happily as he bit off a large chunk of buttered roll.

"There's something about that Roderick I don't like," Dot said flatly.

"Something?" Mary countered, "I don't like any of him. He's all flash suit and smiles, which generally means he'd stab you in the back as soon as look at you. Spencer seems annoyed with him about something as well."

"James doesn't like him either," Pea said.

"The barman?"

"Yep, when we were at the bar I could almost feel the hate coming off him when Roderick spoke to him. Wouldn't surprise me if his boss had given him that black eye."

"And here's another odd one," Dot said in a low voice. Mary turned to see the hotel manager Edward Landry enter with Daisy White in tow.

"So, here we are," he said tersely. "What do you think?"

"It's very nice," Mary said, "lovely ambience." She wasn't entirely sure this made sense in a room with no people, but she thought it sounded like something you should say when complimenting a restaurant.

"We've given the waiting staff the night off today so we'll all be chipping in to look after you, I'll bring out some more champagne to start, I think?" Without waiting for an answer he turned and bustled off towards a door on the far wall which Mary assumed led to the kitchen.

"If you'd like to sit here," Daisy said, gesturing at three seats on one end of a long table before hurrying off back towards the main hotel.

"I don't like champagne," Dot said grumpily when she'd gone and they'd taken their seats, "never have done."

Pea looked at her with a frown. "How can you not like champagne?"

"Oh, don't get her started," Mary said, rolling her eyes. "She'll just go on a rant about bubbles and how they make her burp."

"Well, they do," Dot said haughtily.

"They do that to everyone," Pea laughed. "It doesn't stop it being bloody delicious."

"If he didn't offer us a choice of drinks," Mary pondered, "I wonder if we'll get any say over our dinner."

The door opened again and Edward reappeared with a large bottle of bubbly and three glasses. He was followed by the two young people who worked in the kitchen with the head chef, Anna, Thomas and Ruth.

"Here we are!" Edward said, placing glasses in front of them and pouring a liberal helping in each.

"So, what do you think of Parchester so far?"

Ruth said, taking a seat at the table to the right of Mary.

"To be honest, we've only seen the street from the station to here," she answered, laughing.

"So you've seen it all then," Thomas said in a deadpan voice.

Ruth gave a short, nervous laugh as she glanced at Thomas who was sat on the opposite side of the table. "Don't mind him," Ruth said, rolling her eyes. "He's just got a grump on today."

"One of those days is it?" Pea said cheerfully.

"It's always one of those days here," Thomas said, taking a large swig of champagne.

"Maybe you should go back to the kitchen, Thomas?" Edward said. His lips were curled in a smile that hadn't reached his eyes, which were staring at Thomas rather pointedly.

"Actually, I think I'll stay here a bit longer," Thomas said in a defiant voice, leaning back in his chair.

"I think Anna might need you," Edward continued, his tone insistent.

"So what's new?" Thomas answered, smiling back at him as though challenging him over something.

Edward looked around the table and, seemingly

lost for words, turned and headed back to the kitchen.

Mary stared at the strong, stubbled jaw of Thomas, his blonde hair pushed back over his head into a messy quiff. He looked as though he had stepped off the cover of a fashion magazine rather than someone who worked in a hotel restaurant. Mary's thoughts turned to the blackmailer. Here was someone who clearly seemed less enchanted with life at the hotel than the rest of the staff. She decided to poke this particular hornet's nest and see what flew out.

"How long have you worked here, Thomas?" she said in what she hoped was a conversational tone.

"I came in when Spencer and Roderick bought the place. The same time as Anna and Ruth."

"Ah, so it's actually the three of you that make up the dream team that won Michelin star then?" Mary smiled.

For the first time since she had met the young man, she saw him smile. "I guess you could say that," he looked at Ruth who was returning his gaze with a worried expression. "What do you say, Ruth? Are the three of us some kind of dream team?"

She opened her mouth to reply, closed it again as she looked around at her audience and then finally replied with, "We each bring different skills to the table," she said firmly.

"Some of us just bring one to the table though, eh?" Thomas countered.

There was the briefest moment of tense silence before the door to the hotel opened and Spencer burst through it laughing with Daisy and Roderick in tow.

"And here they all are!" he cried as he saw the group around the table, "No Edward or Anna though I see? No doubt she's in the kitchen working her magic and Edward is fussing around about something."

"Come on," Ruth said to Thomas, rising from her chair. "Everyone's here now, let's go and finish up."

Thomas very deliberately refilled his glass before rising and heading back to the kitchen with it in hand. A worried-looking Ruth followed him, looking back over her shoulder at the group as she went.

"Something I said you think?" Spencer laughed as he sat down. He had clearly continued to enjoy the hotel bar in their absence. His cheeks flushed red and his nose had taken on a vaguely purple hue.

"I think they just needed to get back to the kitchen," Dot said diplomatically.

"Yes, well. I'm bloody starving!" Spencer said as he landed heavily in the chair next to Dot. As if in answer to his prayers, Edward appeared from the kitchen door with a flourish and announced that dinner would soon be served. The delicious smells that wafted from the kitchen after made Mary's stomach growl in anticipation as she suddenly realised she was famished.

CHAPTER SEVEN

As one, the group around the table laid back, most of them with their hands upon their stomachs as though that would aid with the digestion of the meal they had just eaten.

"That was fantastic," Pea said, for what Mary was sure was at least the fourth time since placing the last forkful in his mouth. "Really good," he muttered before burping quietly.

The dinner had passed pleasantly enough, and the food had been excellent. Mary had struggled to find the time to eat in-between answering the many questions that had been fired at her from around the table, but mostly from the enthusiastic and smiling Ruth who seemed to have no end of interest in the world of show business. Mary had eaten the delicious array of small, tapas-style dishes in-between relaying stories to her insatiable audience. Now she felt exhausted. Although the attention had been focused on her, she had been using the opportunity to watch the rest of the group.

Firstly, there was Anna Crosby. Thomas's previous comment about wine now made sense. She was clearly sloshed and had laid down the dishes she carried with a thump that had rattled the glassware. Once seated, she had only nibbled at the food while generously refilling her champagne glass at every opportunity. Thomas was sitting next to her, and Mary couldn't help notice that the anger the young man so clearly had bubbling inside him appeared to be directed towards his boss. Every time Anna had spoken in answer to a question, he had rolled his eyes or angrily stabbed at the food on his plate. His entire demeanour was almost the opposite of his colleague Ruth, who chatted excitedly and beamed her engaging smile almost continuously.

Spencer Harley was also enjoying the alcohol and had grown quiet as the meal had worn on. A consequence, Mary pondered, that might have been due to the whispered conversations that he was still having with his business partner Roderick Sutton who sat next to him. Roderick joined in the overall conversation, laughed at the right moments, made interesting and insightful remarks. All the time though, his attention would return to Spencer and those whispered conversations which had angered Spencer in the bar, but now seemed to have made him quiet and melancholy.

The hotel manager Edward Landry used every opportunity to praise the hotel and enthuse about its future, even when the topic of conversation had not been even remotely related. Daisy had spent the meal gazing at Ruth with a look of almost wonder. It was clear the young girl looked up to her bright and personable colleague and hung off her every word. For the most part, Pea and Dot had remained quiet. Partly because it was clear that the focus was on Mary as the celebrity guest of honour, partly so they could get on with the enjoyable task of trying every dish.

"I'll just go and get coffees," Ruth said standing.

"Oh, let me help you," Mary said quickly as she rose too.

"Oh no!" Edward cried, jumping up. "We can't have our guest of honour making coffee!"

"Nonsense," Mary said, waving him to sit again. "After all, this is supposed to be a night for the staff as well, least I can do. Though I will need some help," she said to Ruth as she moved around the table and took her arm. "I don't have a clue how to use those fancy coffee machines with all the steam and things!"

Ruth laughed and squeezed her arm as they headed through the kitchen door.

They entered a space larger than Mary had expected. Every surface was made of gleaming metal and didn't bear any signs that a meal had even been cooked there.

"Wow, how did you make all that food and leave the kitchen looking like this?!" she said in astonishment.

"Oh, we always clear up as we go," Ruth smiled as she began fiddling with the large coffee machine that was set on a table to their right. "It's one of Thomas's rules."

"Thomas's?"

Mary noticed Ruth's hands hesitate for a moment before continuing. "Well, he's a bit of a clean freak is Thomas. Anna goes along with it," she said with a light laugh.

Mary waited for a moment, but no more information seemed to be forthcoming, so she decided to probe further.

"Anna seems like a nice woman."

"Oh, she's great. Very sweet."

"And she's obviously a fantastic chef, you must be learning a lot from her?"

"Oh, yes."

Mary frowned as she watched her pouring ground coffee into the filter. For someone so enthusiastic about almost everything she spoke about, she was strangely non committal about her boss's skills.

"Is there something going on with Anna and Thomas? I notice he seems pretty ticked off with her."

Ruth turned from the machine to look at her. "We've just had a bit of tension in the kitchen recently, that's all. You know how it is, leading up to a big event and all that."

"Of course," Mary said, unconvinced.

Ruth began an explanation of how the coffee machine worked, whether as a distraction or because making coffee was yet another thing that Ruth Faulkner enthused about, she couldn't tell.

They carried the coffee back into the restaurant where Pea was apparently relating the story of their treasure hunt and discovery of the lost Fabergé egg. Mary smiled as she listened to the wild and embellished version he gave and laughed as she saw Dot's expression. One raised eyebrow, she sat, arms folded, glaring at him disapprovingly.

"And there it was," Pea said proudly, enjoying

the attention, "just sitting there in the wall for all those years."

Mary and Ruth passed out the coffees and jugs of cream as the table offered their congratulations and expressions of amazement at the story.

She watched as Edward Landry passed the milk around until his arm bumped into Thomas Mosley's who was reaching for the sugar bowl, spilling a small trail of milk across the table cloth.

"For goodness sake!" Edward cried, dabbing at the spillage with a napkin.

"Oh, pull that stick out of your arse for once Edward and relax," Thomas retorted, laughing as he dropped a sugar cube into his coffee and began to stir. There was a series of hushed conversations from the staff's end of the table before the conversation broke out into smaller groups and for the first time since the meal had been brought out, Mary felt as though she had a chance to talk to her friends. Their position at one end of the table allowing them at least some privacy as the others chatted and bickered.

"So, anything?"

"Well the food was lovely," Pea said earnestly.

"She means about the case," Dot snapped, digging him in the ribs with her elbow.

"Ow!" Pea frowned, rubbing his chest.

"I feel like there's a lot going on around the table

that isn't being spoken about," Dot answered Mary with a knowing look.

"I get that impression as well, but I guess that's partly to be expected. When people work with each other for a long time you can get on each other's nerves."

"Oh," Dot said in surprise. "I had no idea you were aware of how annoying you are to work with."

"I was referring to you," Mary said, smiling sweetly back at her.

Spencer stood up, scraping his chair back on the floor noisily before clearing his throat. "Shall we all go through to the bar for a nightcap?" he asked in a hopeful voice.

The group rose with murmurs of agreement.

"Let's not worry about all this," Ruth said gesturing to the table and at Anna and Thomas. "I'll sort it all in the morning."

"Thanks, Ruth," Thomas said quietly, even managing a smile. Mary noticed that he had a kind of waxy sheen to his skin, which she assumed was from alcohol. Anna said nothing but smiled as she tottered unsteadily towards the door which led back into the hotel, looking even more worse-for-wear than her employee.

"She likes a drink, that one," Dot said. Mary had heard that tone of disapproval in her voice before, but it was nice for it to be directed at someone else for a change.

"Yes, I think there's something going on with the kitchen staff," Mary answered in a low whisper as they entered the short passageway which led back to the hotel. "I tried to get something out of Ruth when we were making the coffee, but for someone so chatty she went strangely quiet."

"Hey!" Pea called in a stage whisper from behind them. They turned to see him gesturing at them to move back to the restaurant. They hurried back as he put his finger to his lips and opened the door a crack. Edward Landry and Thomas Moseley stood facing each other, and despite their lowered voices, clearly arguing.

"I know what you're planning to do Thomas," Edward growled, "and I won't stand for it!"

"Don't you think you've all drawn enough blood from me?" Thomas snapped back. "I know you all like to keep this little delusion that we're all a happy family and that the hotel is going to turn around, but face it. This place is as dead as the town is and I deserve more than that."

"You ungrateful little sod!" Edward roared, clearly forgetting to keep his voice down now. "We gave you a chance when no one else would touch you!"

"But that won't be the case for long, will it? Soon everyone will see the truth, and I can't wait to see what you do then!" Thomas turned towards them and the three eavesdroppers stumbled over each other as they turned and dashed down the hall towards the lobby before he reached the door. As they emerged from the hallway, they began to walk slowly again, moving towards the bar in as natural a manner as they could muster.

"What on earth was all that about?!" Pea said quietly.

"I have no idea," Mary answered, "but I think finding a blackmailer amongst this lot might be difficult. Half of them seem to be at each other's throats as it is!" She opened the door to the bar and held it as Thomas appeared from the restaurant behind them. He walked slowly towards her, the waxy look of his skin even more apparent than before, but the colour had also drained from his face.

"Are you ok Thomas?" Mary asked as she reached the door.

He looked at her in what appeared to be a state of confusion. He tried to speak, but no words were discernible. Instead, his tongue seemed to flop around his mouth as though he had no control over it as his eyes widened in distress.

"Someone get some water!" Mary shouted into

the bar as she helped him through, putting his arm over her shoulder. He stumbled, and she was only just able to take his weight. Pea dashed from the bar and took the other side as they eased him into a seat.

"What's wrong with him?" Pea said in horror at the strange expression on the young man's face.

"I have no idea!" Mary said, staring at Thomas's normally handsome features. They seemed to have drooped somehow, as though his skin and muscle had become elastic. "Maybe it's a stroke?" Mary said quietly to Pea whites shrugged.

The others had gathered around now, and James the barman had arrived with a glass of water and a jug to refill it. Mary took it and moved to Thomas's lips, but he just spluttered and sent it spraying over her. Behind her she could hear Roderick calling an ambulance as Thomas suddenly shook violently, his body spasming in jerks as he cried out in pain. She was vaguely aware of people shouting around her, screaming even, but everything was background. She was staring into the eyes of a man who was fighting for his life, and the world around her had all but vanished. She held his hand tightly.

"Help is coming," she said to him, leaning closer. "You're going to be OK."

His eyes flickered as he shook with another jolt of pain and began to retch. She turned him over the side of the chair just in time for a small pool of yellow bile to spill from his slack lips to the floor before his entire body went rigid for a full three seconds and then collapsed back into the seat his eyes still open, but now, unseeing.

CHAPTER EIGHT

F or Mary, the next couple of hours were a blur of chaos, confusion and sadness. People talked to her, or at least at her. Others shouted, others cried. Thomas Mosley was dead at the age of just twenty-four, and it had happened right in front of them. There was talk of an underlying heart condition, of medication, of the stress of tomorrow's event and the long hours worked pushing his heart to the point of failure. Mary didn't believe any of it.

Almost as soon as the light had faded from the eyes of the young man she had cradled in her arms, she had lifted her phone and dialled a number. She had done it automatically, all her previous doubts about calling the number gone in the wake of this tragedy. Inspector Joe Corrigan had answered with a light and playful tone. If Mary had not been in a dazed state, she might have noted that he seemed pleased she had called. Instead, she said two simple sentences.

"I need you to come to the Rudolph Hotel in Parchester. A man's been murdered."

There had been only the smallest moment of hesitation before he answered, "I'm on my way."

Now, forty minutes later, she saw him as he came through the doors of the hotel and into the lobby where they were all gathered. His dark eyes seeking her out as a uniformed officer filled him in on what had happened. As soon as his eyes met hers, he moved towards her, the young police officer having to jog behind to continue his update.

He slowed as he reached Mary, his brown eyes searching hers. His hand rose up and touched her arm.

"Are you OK?"

Mary nodded, blinking away the tears which had begun to build in her eyes. "He was murdered Joe, I'm sure of it."

He nodded back at her. "I'll look into it," he said, and she believed him. He turned away from her and moved towards the door of the bar area, which had been cleared by all except the police.

"Are you sure you should be saying that?" Pea said from her side. Mary suddenly felt more like her old self and turned on him with a thunderous expression.

"I've told you, there is no way that man died of a heart attack," she said in a quiet but firm voice.

"But come on, Mary," Pea said warily. He had seen enough of Mary's temper over the years to know that now was a time to tread carefully. "He had a dodgy heart, everyone here at the hotel knew it."

"All that means is that whoever did it knew that he would be an easy target to be poisoned."

Pea sighed and looked to Dot for support.

"I think she might have a point," Dot said in a level voice.

"Seriously?!" Pea whined, putting his hand on his head.

"I saw a man having a heart attack once," Dot said thoughtfully. "I was queueing at the fish and chip shop, and the chap in front of me just keeled over. I can tell you now, it wasn't anything like what happened here. It might have been his heart that gave out in the end, but there was something else going on before it, I'm sure."

"Thank you," Mary said, squeezing her shoulder. Dot wasn't someone who would side with someone just because they needed to hear it. She would always say what she really thought. It was one of the qualities that endeared her to Mary, why considered herself as someone who needed the harsh reality of truth spoken to her occasionally in order to keep her on the straight and narrow.

"Ok," Pea said, sighing. "Let's say you're right. How on earth could it even have happened?! I mean, we all ate the same food. Thomas even helped make it! It seems pretty unlikely that he could have been poisoned without anyone else getting sick."

Mary looked over his shoulder at the small group of people they had shared a meal with that night, her eyes focusing on Spencer Harley. "This has to be something to do with the blackmail letter," she said thoughtfully. "It can't be a coincidence."

"You think whoever is blackmailing Spencer was also blackmailing Thomas over something?"

Mary shrugged. "Who knows, but I guess if you've taken the step to blackmail someone once, you might well do it again. We need to talk to Spencer, he's got to tell us more after this, surely?"

"Why hasn't he told us more already?" Dot said, "I mean, he invited you here to look into it all and yet he doesn't seem to want to talk about it much or show us these letters he's received."

"What are you saying?" Pea asked, frowning. It was Dot's turn to shrug.

"Maybe he was making it up?" Mary said quietly.

All three of them turned to stare at the large figure of Spencer Harley.

"But why on earth would he do that?" Pea asked.

Spencer looked up from the conversation he was having with the group and saw the three of them looking at him. He extracted himself from his group and made his way across to them.

"How are you all doing?" he said, appearing far soberer than he did earlier, but Mary noted he still had a drink in hand. "I'm terribly sorry you have had to go through this, terrible business."

"What was this heart condition he had?" Mary asked.

"Oh, no idea. Just knew he had a dodgy ticker. I think Ruth and Anna know more about it, but it doesn't matter much now, eh?" He looked at Mary, his brow furrowed in concern. "There's was nothing you or anyone else could have done I'm sure."

"How is Edward taking it?"

"Edward?" Spencer looked back towards the group of hotel staffed. "Seems OK, why do you ask?"

"We saw him arguing with Thomas just before it happened. I'd imagine he was feeling a little guilty if that's what caused Thomas to... have his problem."

"Oh, well, he never said anything. Still, we've all had arguments from time to time, you certainly don't expect the other chap to drop dead."

"You don't think this could have anything to do with the letters you received?"

Spencer's eyes widened as he looked around them frantically. "Please, I don't think we need to bring that up to the police. This is just one of those tragic things that happen, nothing to do with my letters."

Mary stared back at him. She could feel the eyes of her brother and friend on her as well, they were letting her take the lead. Dot, because that was what she did, Pea because he doubted her version of events. Either way, she wasn't going to back down.

"I think Thomas was poisoned," she said bluntly.

Spencer gaped at her. "You can't be serious." He looked at Pea and Dot, but the blank expressions on their faces offered him no comfort. "The young chap had a heart condition, and why on earth would anyone poison him?! I must say, Mary, when I invited you here I thought you might be able to help in what is a very delicate manner, now I see that all this detective stuff in the press has gone to your head! Seeing poisoners and murderers everywhere!"

In his shock at the suggestion, his voice had risen and now everyone in the lobby was looking at them. It was Ruth Faulkner who broke away from the hotel group first, hurrying over to them with a wild look in her already red eyes.

"You think Thomas was poisoned?!" she said, grasping Mary's arm and bringing her face close to hers.

"Yes," Mary said, aware that the rest of the hotel staff were making their way over, all eyes on her. "There was something strange going on before his heart gave out, you all saw it." She looked around the group, who stood in stunned silence. "I think Thomas Mosley was murdered."

_____

CHAPTER NINE

"You're not one to keep your head down are you?" Inspector Joe Corrigan said to Mary when they were seated at a table in the corner of the bar. "You've got half of uniform talking about how the TV detective has been in too many shows and now is seeing murder everywhere."

"What did the pathologist say?" Mary said sharply. She was in no mood for small-talk.

"Well, she didn't say anything about poisoning if that's what you're asking. She looked him over, but she won't know anything until she gets him back and looks properly."

'You are treating this as suspicious, though?"

"I am because for some reason I believe you have good instincts for this sort of thing, but I can't launch a full murder investigation without more evidence.

Thomas Mosley had an erratic heartbeat. You were all present at the meal he ate, and he even cooked his own food. I'd have a hard time persuading anyone to give me the resources to pursue it."

He watched as Mary visibly sagged in front of him, her eyes scanning the surface of the small table between them. She looked up at him sharply. "What if we looked into it? Could you help us unofficially?"

His brow furrowed, but at the same time, his mouth rose at one corner. "You've got a taste for it, haven't you?"

Mary folded her arms. "This isn't a game."

"No," he said, his expression hardening, "It isn't. If you're right, then it could be a very dangerous situation. If someone killed this young man, they won't hesitate to do so again in order to cover it up, and if you start asking questions and poking around, who knows what will happen."

"I understand the risks," Mary said her chin lifted defiantly, "but what's the alternative here? If I'm right, and we don't do anything, we could be letting someone get away with murder."

Corrigan took a deep breath and leaned back in his chair. His penetrating, deep brown eyes held Mary in their gaze until she began to feel uncomfortable before he spoke.

"I can get the food tested," he said in a low voice.

"It will be off the books, but I can call in a favour at the lab. There will be a postmortem in any case, and I'll have a word with the pathologist to look for signs of poisoning. That's about all I can do, though. You'll pretty much be on your own."

"I have Dot and Pea," Mary said confidently.

She saw Corrigan's gaze turn to his left and followed his line of sight. Dot and Pea were sat at the bar, Dot stirring her drink thoughtfully and Pea throwing peanuts into the air to catch them in his mouth. One landed in his eye and he gave a squeal of pain.

"For some reason," Corrigan continued, turning back towards her, "that doesn't fill me with confidence."

"I can call you if I need a knight in shining armour," she said sarcastically.

"Well, my armour's a bit rusty, but I'll be there if you need me."

Mary felt herself blush and quickly stood up. "Right, well I'll be in touch," she said quickly.

"See you soon, Mary," he said, also rising. "And be careful."

"I'm not completely helpless, you know," she snapped before turning away and heading for the bar.

Why did he drive her so crazy?

She quickly buried the thought for fear of the answer and instead took her annoyance out on Pea.

"Can you stop throwing peanuts around?" she snapped. "You look like a bloody idiot."

"I take it your chat with the lovely detective went well then?" Dot said in what Mary considered was a rather malevolent tone.

"Fine actually," she retorted, hopping onto a stool next to her old friend. "He's agreed that we can look into the poisoning."

"And why would he do, that?" Pea asked, smarting somewhat from the idiot comment.

"Because he believes me," Mary said simply. "And because he can't investigate himself as there isn't enough to go on."

"Right," Dot said with a deep breath. "Where do we start?"

"We start by getting Spencer to show us those blackmail letters," Mary said, hopping to her feet again. "Come on."

She marched out of the bar and up the stairs towards the highest floor of the hotel where she knew Spencer's rooms to be. He had retired for the evening along with the other staff who were at dinner, all of whom were staying at the hotel for their big event the next day. It hadn't yet been cancelled, but Spencer had insisted it would be in the morning.

She rapped on the door and was surprised to hear an immediately barked answer from the other side.

"I've told you I'm not speaking about it anymore tonight!" Spencer's voice boomed.

"Spencer? It's me, Mary."

There was a moment of silence before the door gently opened to reveal a red-faced Spencer.

"Mary? Sorry, my dear, thought you were someone else."

"Who exactly?"

He looked at her and then Dot and Pea who stood behind her.

"Can I help you with something? If there's a problem with your rooms, it's really Edward you need to speak to..."

"No," Mary said, pushing past him and entering the room, "we just wanted a little chat with you."

"Oh, right," Spencer burbled as Dot and Pea marched past him as well. He closed the door with a resigned look on his face. "It's not still this silly poisoning idea, is it?" he said as he slumped into an armchair that sat by a dressing table.

The room was larger than Mary's and had the feel of being someone's personal space rather than a hotel room. Various newspapers and books were strewn across the dressing table and a bookcase which Mary was sure wasn't regulation hotel issue, had been transformed into an open drinks cabinet.

"I'm afraid it is the 'silly' poisoning thing," Mary said harshly,

"I'd have thought you would be a little more interested in the idea bearing in mind the letters you've been receiving," Pea added.

"I told you all before! This has nothing to do with those letters!"

"Then why don't you show them to us and we won't keep bothering you about them," Dot said.

"I can't," Spencer blustered, "I threw the things out as soon as they arrived."

"You threw them out?!" Pea asked, incredulous. "Why on earth would you do that?! They were evidence!"

There was a moment's pause before Mary spoke quietly. "Maybe that's just it, maybe they revealed some evidence that whoever wrote them thought you'd be willing to pay to keep quiet."

Spencer visibly sagged. "You're right of course." He sighed. "I didn't want to show the police them, or you. I knew questions would be asked. And everything would be ruined."

"Did Thomas write the letters?" Mary continued.

Spencer looked up at her. "What do you mean,

Thomas? Why do you say that?" His face clouded in anger. "You don't mean you think I've killed the poor chap because of these blasted letters do you?! I'd have sooner given in to their demands! I'd never kill anyone!"

"Their demands?" Mary frowned. "You mean they weren't asking you for money?"

Spencer sighed again as he poured himself another drink from the whiskey bottle that sat on the table next to him.

"The truth is, I know who's sending me the letters, and no, they weren't asking for money. Look," he said, leaning forward, "when I saw that you had been involved in solving a murder case Mary, I just thought I could get you along here and get you to dig up the evidence on who was sending them somehow. Then I could deal with it discreetly, maybe." He took another gulp and stared at the glass in his hand.

"So," Dot said after it became clear that he had finished talking, "if it wasn't Thomas, who was it? And what did they want if they didn't want money?"

"They want me to sell the hotel," he said in a bitter tone. "We've been approached by a development company that wants to turn the place into flats."

"And what does Roderick think of this?" Pea said. "He owns half, doesn't he?"

"Actually," Mary said before Spencer could respond, "I think Spencer means that Roderick might well be the ones sending the letters."

Spencer gave a small laugh. "See, I knew you were the right woman for the job, though it's a bit late now I suppose."

"What do you mean by that?"

"The hotel is a bit of a disaster to tell you the truth, costs more money to keep the thing standing upright than it brings in. I doubt someone dying here is going to bring the punters in, and on top of that we've lost one-third of the kitchen staff that made the only profitable part tick!"

"The restaurant," Mary said thoughtfully. "Surely Anna will be able to carry on eventually though, she's the head chef."

Mary noticed a flicker of something pass across Spencer's face at the mention of Anna Crosby. "Can I ask why you don't want to sell?" she said.

"Well, I couldn't do it to Anna, not when everything's going so well, and then there's young Daisy of course. She would be devastated if the place became flats after her father worked here all those years."

Mary felt as though she had scored a hit, but tried not to let it show.

"So Roderick has been pestering you to sell.

That's what you were arguing about earlier at the bar?"

He nodded. "Bloody chap won't stop going on about it, that's how I know he sent the letters."

"Did you confront him about it?"

"I... no, I didn't."

"Why not?"

"Look, it's been a long night. Can we talk again in the morning? I'm sure the police will do a thorough job in any case."

Mary thought for a moment, then nodded. "Ok, we'll see you tomorrow Spencer."

"I'm sure you will," he answered glumly.

CHAPTER TEN

W hen Mary woke the next morning, there was a moment where she had no idea where she was. She looked around with bleary eyes at yet another hotel room; she had seen so many in her life, and lay back on the pillow. It was then that the events of the previous evening came flooding back to her. Thomas's face etched in pain as he staggered towards her. The spark of life dying in his eyes before her own. She shuddered and turned her mind to what she now thought of as 'the investigation'.

After their talk with Spencer, they had all ventured back down to the lobby where the police presence was already thinning. Corrigan had been right when he said there was little he could do to turn this into a full investigation without evidence of poisoning. She knew that, but it didn't make it any less annoying. They had spoken briefly, he had once again warned her to be careful, and this time it had given her a warm glow to hear him say those words. Even if there was a potential killer on the loose, his first concern was about her. Then Mary, Pea and Dot had retired for bed, all of them drained from the day's events. Mary had slept as she always did, like the dead.

She was showered and dressed in what, for her, might constitute record time. The look on Dot's face when she knocked on her door certainly suggested so.

"Well, I never thought I'd see the day when you were up and out before me."

"Ah!" Mary said dramatically as she moved past her into her room, "But these are different days! We have a murderer to catch!"

"You're not on Her Law now you know, there's no audience to play to here."

"Oh, don't be such a killjoy," Mary admonished as she leaned on the window sill and looked down into the street. Figures dashed about below, scarves wrapped around them to keep out the cold.

"So what's the plan?" Dot said from behind her as she sprayed perfume and then adjusted her hair in the mirror.

Mary turned and frowned at her. She had given

Dot the perfume as a present some years ago, as a way of coaxing out her womanly charms for the world to see. She was sure they were in there somewhere, they were probably just hidden under all the bustle of efficiency and pastel cardigans. In any case, she had never known Dot to wear the scent apart from the last week or so. And now she was adjusting her hair as though she was about to be photographed for stationary monthly (which was the kind of magazine Mary assumed Dot would feature on). She was about to ask what had inspired this change of nature when there was a sharp rap at the door.

Dot moved across to it and opened it to reveal Pea, who was standing with his ginger hair still slicked back from his morning shower. He was wearing a navy blue blazer over a light grey shirt and had a flower in his buttonhole.

"Morning," he said to Dot before double-taking at the sight of Mary behind her. "Blimey Mary, up already?"

"Why is everyone so surprised!" Mary said, rather put out at the implied slur on her character. "And why are you both acting like you're off to Ascot or something?" she said, eyeing his buttonhole.

"I have no idea what you're talking about," Pea said quickly, "but we should get a move on and go downstairs. I've already seen the others going to the restaurant for breakfast." He turned back into the hall and Dot and Mary followed.

"Does the hotel normally do breakfast in the restaurant?" Mary asked as they moved down the stairs.

"Apparently so," Pea said "I had a quick chat with Anna this morning. They don't class it as restaurant work really though, they just do a basic English breakfast that Ruth and Thomas normally knock together."

"What do you make of Anna?" Dot said. "I haven't had a chance to speak to her yet."

"Seems nice enough, quiet sort."

"That doesn't exactly fit in with the image of a chef, does it?" Mary asked.

"I guess they're not all like the shouty, sweaty ones on TV," Dot answered as they reached the lobby.

The large front doors were closed, and there was an almost eerie quiet in the large room.

"Looks like they've closed the hotel up," Mary said.

"Yes, we thought it was best," Edward said suddenly, appearing from behind the staircase and the corridor which led to the restaurant. The hotel manager had the same faint smile his fish lips always seemed to sport and seemed quite unaffected by the events of the previous evening.

"What about the guests?" Dot asked.

"There were only three rooms occupied as of yesterday, they all decided to leave last night after the events that transpired."

"You mean when Thomas was poisoned?" Mary said bluntly.

Those large, puffy lips twitched. "Spencer told me you had some strange idea that foul play was involved," he said slowly. "I assume it was you who persuaded the police to take samples of the food we ate last night?"

"I think the police were just following their own suspicions," Mary lied. If Edward was anything to do with Thomas's death, then she didn't want him to think the idea of murder just her crackpot theory. That could prove dangerous.

"Well," I'm sure they are mistaken. We all know Thomas had a heart condition, it was nothing more than a terrible tragedy. Now, if you'd like to follow me?" He turned and moved back down the corridor.

Mary exchanged glances with Dot and Pea, all of them with eyebrows raised at the flippant manner of the hotel manager, and gave pursuit.

As expected, the restaurant was a quiet and sombre place. The small group that sat at the table looked up at them as they approached with listless expressions. There was a low chorus of good mornings as the three of them took their place at the end of the table.

"I'm afraid there's not much on offer," Ruth said, her bright eyes ringed with dark lines. "Things were a bit difficult in the kitchen this morning." Her eyes flickered across the table to Anna who was staring at her plate, pushing scrambled egg around it with a fork.

"We've decided to cancel tonight's bash," Roderick said from a seat next to Spencer, who was tucking into a sausage with gusto. "It's a shame, but we don't think it would be right to go on."

"Of course," Mary said, pouring herself coffee from a large insulated pot which stood on the table in front of her. "What about Thomas's family, have any of you spoken to them?"

"I have," Ruth said in a hoarse voice, "It was awful, they were just so..." she shook her head and blew her nose loudly on a napkin.

Mary felt a pang of sympathy for the young woman who had seemed so full of life and enthusiasm yesterday and now looked the opposite.

"We've sent them condolences from everyone at the hotel of course," Spencer said, still with a mouthful of sausage. "Just wish we could do more."

Mary noticed Roderick give Spencer a sharp look.

"What do you think's going to happen to the restaurant now?" Daisy said. She looked pale and small, like a field mouse that had emerged, blinking from the hedgerow. James reached out a hand and placed it on hers, but she pulled it away.

"Oh, you know how these things are," Spencer said looking at Anna on the far side of the table. "It's all very sad, but the show must go on. I expect you'll want to be hiring someone new at some point, Anna?"

She looked up suddenly, as though noticing them all in the room for the first time. "I'm sorry, what?"

"I said I'm sure, after a respectable period, you'll be wanting to get someone else in to give you a hand in the kitchen, eh?" Spencer repeated.

Her eyes widened in shock and she bolted upright, knocking her chair over behind her. "No! You don't understand! I can't just replace him! The whole thing's over now!" She turned and ran from the table towards the kitchen.

"She's just upset I'm sure," Ruth said unconvincingly to the rest of the table as she dashed after her.

"Everyone's clearly been under a great deal of strain," Edward said to the three guests in a voice designed to reassure. "Perhaps you'd prefer to eat in peace? I'm sure everyone has things they need to get on with?" He looked pointedly at James and Daisy, who took the hint and rose from the table and headed for the door.

"Yes, and you and I have a meeting, don't we, Spencer?" Roderick said standing. Spencer's face sagged more than it already did naturally.

"Oh, all bloody right man, don't you ever give it a rest?" He stood up and moved around the table until he was next to Mary, Dot and Pea. "Sorry about all this, you're welcome to stay as long as you want at the hotel, of course, go and see what there is of the town and things," he nodded and gave a small, forced smile before following Roderick out the door with Edward behind.

"Well," Pea said, taking a piece of toast from a rack. "Nothing's ever dull around here is it?"

"It's hard to believe that the same person cooked this as the meal last night," Dot said as she cut into an overdone sausage that bounced across her plate.

"You saw the state of Anna though," Mary said sipping at her coffee, "she doesn't exactly look like someone in the right frame of mind."

"True," Dot answered. "To be honest, this whole place seems bloody strange if you ask me."

"How do you mean?" Mary asked, head tilting as

she tried to ignore Pea who was cramming a large mouthful of egg and sausage into his mouth.

"This hotel, I mean, it's clearly a disaster. There are hardly any guests, hardly any staff. Didn't Spencer say that he and Roderick bought it two years ago? What on earth have they been doing? It's obviously not making them any money."

"I guess that's what they've been bickering about since we've been here," Mary said. "Roderick wants to sell up because the place is a disaster and Spencer doesn't want to."

Dot eyes her suspiciously. "You said that as though you know why he doesn't want to sell, what is it?"

"I just noticed the way Spencer talks about Anna, I think there's something there."

"Spencer has a thing for Anna?!" Pea said as he bit into a piece of toast. "Well, that would explain things. He doesn't want to sell up and turf her out of the place just when it's going well for her, does he?"

"It does look like Roderick was the one sending the letters," Dot said. "I don't know why Spencer didn't just accuse him and get it over and done with."

"There must have been something in those letters that meant he didn't want to risk telling Roderick if he'd got it wrong and he wasn't the blackmailer," Mary said, sitting up excitedly. "That's why he wanted me to come to try to find some evidence for who was sending them!"

"Makes sense," Pea nodded. "I still don't see why anyone would kill Thomas, though. What's he got to do with any of this?"

"Maybe he found out that Roderick wanted to sell and he decided to keep him quiet?" Mary said unconvincingly.

"A bit weak."

"Yes, Pea, I'm well aware of that thank you," Mary answered before draining her coffee. "You two stay here, I'm going to go and check on whether Anna is alright and I think she's more likely to talk if it's just me." They both nodded in agreement. They had seen how shy and quiet the head chef was, just as Mary had.

Mary walked towards the kitchen to the sounds of Dot complaining about Pea talking with his mouthful and smiled as a thought occurred to her.

CHAPTER ELEVEN

The kitchen was a startlingly bright space of white brick and metal sheeting. Spotlights covered the ceiling and were angled at various points on the metal workbenches which were littered with various bits of apparatus from this morning's breakfast, in sharp contrast to the cleanliness after last night's meal. For the first time, it occurred to Mary that if she really thought Thomas had been poisoned, having breakfast made in the same kitchen by the same people as made his last meal might not have been the wisest move. At least she had stuck to coffee in the face of the rather sub-par spread. Pea, on the other hand, would be dead before lunch the way he had gone at it. She decided to put the matter from her mind as she approached Anna who was sat on a chair at a small wooden table to the back of the room with Ruth opposite her, holding her hands.

"Everything alright?" she said, feeling as though she needed to announce herself in what looked like a personal moment between friends.

They both turned towards her with glistening eyes.

"We've all just had a bit of a shock," Ruth said. "I think it's only just hitting us, really."

"Of course," Mary said sitting in the remaining empty chair. "I can't imagine how you must all be feeling having worked so closely together."

"It's very difficult," Ruth said, looking at Anna.

"Can I make you a cup of tea or anything?"

"No, thank you," Anna said, speaking for the first time in a small voice.

"I always think, when we lose someone, that the best thing to do is remember all the good times you had with them. Tell me about Thomas."

"I'm not sure that now is the right time," Ruth said uncertainly, but Anna began speaking, her eyes glazed over.

"He was such a wonderful cook," she said quietly. "It was like he had magic in his fingers that could turn any ingredients into something fabulous. Now he'll never cook again."

Mary watched the woman's face carefully. Her

high forehead seemed even paler than normal against her dark hair. Her wide mouth was pinched with sadness.

"Never mind though," Ruth said, leaning across the table towards her boss. "We can make sure he lives on, can't we?"

"What do you mean?" Mary asked, making Ruth's head snap back to her as though she had momentarily forgotten she was there.

"I just mean through our cooking," she said quickly. "I think you could do with a lie down upstairs Anna."

"Yes," Anna said meekly. "You're probably right."

Ruth smiled at Mary as she walked back out of the kitchen, her arm around Anna's shoulders.

Mary looked around the kitchen but found nothing much of interest. She wasn't sure exactly what she had been looking for. It was unlikely the police would have missed a large jar marked 'poison', but still, she was disappointed. There were three distinct work areas, that much was obvious. There was a large space that was meticulously arranged with hanging utensils above. She assumed that was where Anna worked. Either side were smaller areas. One had a picture of Ruth and Anna smiling outside the hotel above it, so she assumed that was Ruth's. She moved to the other one, but it was devoid of anything personal. Just equipment in drawers and practical wipe clean surfaces to work on. She sighed and headed back into the restaurant.

"What on earth did you say to those two?" Pea said as she returned to the table. "They both came through here as though they'd seen a ghost!"

"I just asked about Thomas," Mary shrugged. "They found it hard, obviously, but Anna is acting as though the whole restaurant is never going to run again."

"Well, we have some gossip for you as well!" Pea said, grinning from ear to ear.

"Go on," Mary said eagerly.

"Well, Dot here, being the brainy type she is, suggested that someone could have come in from the street side and somehow got the poison into Thomas's food that way."

"Right," Mary said slightly disappointed. This seemed about as unlikely as any theory she had thought of herself, but not yet shared.

"Oh, I know it's silly," Dot said defensively, reading her look. "I just think it's a good idea to look into every possibility."

'Quite right," Pea nodded. "No stone unturned and all that."

"Can you just cut to the bit where you tell me something interesting?" Mary said.

"Right, well, we popped outside to see if there were any CCTV cameras. Good thinking, eh?" Pea waggled his eyebrows at her.

"Yes, good dog, have a biscuit,"

"There's no need to be like that," Pea said, looking hurt. "Anyway, we wandered down the street a bit and then Dot here pulls me into the doorway of a fire exit."

"Did she now?" Mary looked at Dot, who steadfastly refused to return her gaze.

"Yes, because the clever thing had spotted Edward Landry talking to James Donavon!"

"Ok," Mary answered slowly, not seeing what was so strange about the hotel manager talking to one of his staff.

"They had ducked around the corner from the hotel," Pea carried on enthusiastically. "We just got out of sight in time and we heard what they were saying! Well, most of it."

"Which was?"

"Edward was telling James that they all had to stick together no matter what and make sure the hotel kept going."

"Nothing unusual about that," Mary said frowning. "It sounds like he's just trying to keep morale up or whatever."

"But then James said, 'you don't think she could

have done it, do you?', just like that! And his face looked like someone had drained the blood from him."

Mary felt a rush of excitement. "So he obviously suspects someone!" She flopped back into the seat she had been hovering over. "What did Edward say to that?"

"He said, 'Don't be silly, what would she have to gain?' And then walked off, but James looked liked he'd had his face slapped."

"He looked confused to me," Dot chimed in for the first time in this tale, "like he suddenly didn't know what Edward was talking about."

"Which might mean he thinks this woman did have something to gain from Thomas's death."

"Any ideas?" Pea asked hopefully. "We can't work it out. I mean, there's only three to choose from: Anna, Ruth and Daisy. But we can't see what help getting Thomas out of the way would do for any of them."

"No, me either," Mary answered, deep in thought, but I've talked to the other two, I might as well go and find the third."

CHAPTER TWELVE

Mary approached the open cupboard and rapped on the door. There was a shout of surprise and the sound of a mop bucket skidding across the floor as she leaned her head around the door and saw Daisy White, whose name currently matched her skin colour.

"Sorry," Mary said quickly, holding her hands out. "I didn't mean to make you jump!"

"It's OK," Daisy said, looking flustered as she righted the mop and dusted herself down. "It's just, with everything that's happened I'm a bit on edge."

"Of course. How are you doing?"

"Oh, OK, trying to keep myself busy you know." She gestured to the large cupboard whose shelves were lined with cleaning products.

"Surely you're not cleaning today?"

"Oh, no. Just checking how much of things we've got left, that kind of thing." She looked at Mary, her plain, rounded face looking unsure. "Do you really think someone might have poisoned Thomas?"

"Yes," Mary said firmly. "Can you think of anyone that might want to have done that?"

"No! He was so nice and everyone said he was excellent in the kitchen. I'm sure it was just that condition he had."

"So he got on with everyone at the hotel?"

"Oh yes, everyone liked him." She smiled coyly. "He was good looking and he knew it, a bit full of himself, but charming with it." She smiled, and then it faded as her eyes filled with tears.

"I'm sorry, I know this must be hard for you. What about Anna and Ruth, did they all get on in the kitchen?"

"Oh yeah, those three were as thick as thieves. They never let anyone else in the kitchen when they were working."

Mary sighed, feeling as though she wasn't getting anywhere. "And what do you think will happen to the restaurant now?"

"Oh, I'm sure they'll be alright. After all, Anna's the star attraction, isn't she? And the hotel needs it if we're going to turn this place around."

"You really care for this place, don't you?" Mary said smiling.

"I love it," Daisy said warmly. "I basically grew up in the hotel when dad worked here, it's always felt like home."

"What about James?" Mary asked, hoping that just saying the barman's name might provoke some kind of reaction.

"James?" Daisy answered, her cheeks colouring. "I don't know what you mean," she said with a small shake of her head.

Mary scrambled for something to say and suddenly remembered James's hand reaching out for Daisy's at breakfast before the young woman had pulled it away.

"I thought there might be something between you two?"

Daisy's brow furrowed and her lips thinned. "No, there's nothing between us."

There was something angry behind this statement, but before she could push it further, a movement to her right made Mary look up and she saw Ruth Faulkner exiting from a room and heading towards the stairs.

"I'll see you later," Mary said quickly and turned to jog after Ruth. Her previous conversation with the young cook had not revealed much, but that had been in front of Anna, her boss. Maybe a one-on-one conversation would be more enlightening.

Away from Anna Crosby, Ruth Faulkner seemed to have regained her sprightly nature.

"Oh! Hello Mary. Sorry about all that before, I think Anna is just a bit shocked, of course, we all are!"

"Yes, of course," Mary said, following her through the door at the end of the corridor and down the stairs. "I was wondering if you could just tell me more about Thomas?"

"What do you want to know?" Ruth asked in a light tone.

"Well, what was he like? Who were his friends?"

"He knocked around with some lads from school." She shrugged. "He was pretty focused on his work though, so he wasn't much of a socialite."

"He cared about his work then?"

She gave a light laugh. "You could say that! Thomas was obsessed with cooking, it was his whole life. He had so many plans." She shook her head sadly as she stopped in the middle of the empty lobby and stared at the floor. "I guess all we can do is try and carry on as he would have wanted," she said, snapping out of it and looking up with a bright smile. "The restaurant, I mean. Anyway, I better go. I said

I'd help make some calls about cancelling things tonight."

Mary watched her head off towards the restaurant and folded her arms. Why did she get the feeling that everyone here was not being honest with her?

She pulled her coat on, wrapped her scarf around her and headed out of the main doors of the hotel. She turned right, walking towards the centre of Parchester where she had earlier agreed to meet Dot and Pea. As she reached the corner, she glanced right into the side street that the restaurant faced out onto and saw a middle-aged couple staring through the glass front. Something about their manner made her pause. They were so still, so quiet, that she somehow knew instinctively who they were.

They turned towards her as she approached them.

"Hi, are you Thomas's parents?"

"That's right," the man nodded. "I'm Geoff and this is Karen."

"I'm so sorry for your loss," Mary said quietly.

He nodded as tears rolled down his wife's cheeks.

"I've just been hearing what a fantastic cook he was."

Geoff gave a small chuckle as Karen smiled. "Oh yes!" Geoff laughed. "He was very ambitious was

Thomas. He was going to go right to the top, you know, this place was just a starting point."

"He planned to leave?"

"Oh yes, he'd already had an offer from a restaurant in London."

"Very prestigious place," Karen chimed in.

"Yes, very prestigious," Geoff confirmed. The two of them looked back at the restaurant and the moment of joy at remembering their son had turned to sadness at his loss again.

"I really am sorry," she said again, but they didn't seem to hear her. They stared into the restaurant holding hands, tears falling silently onto the street at their feet.

CHAPTER THIRTEEN

"He was going to leave?" Pea said in surprise.

"It sounds like it," Mary answered, biting into her panini with gusto.

She had found Pea and Dot back in the small café on the High street through the town, that they had been to yesterday. The smell of melted cheese had assaulted her senses upon entering and reminded her that she had not eaten at breakfast. Before she had even said hello to them she had ordered a ham and cheese panini, a large latté and a chocolate brownie, and was now attacking the melted masterpiece with enthusiasm. She was glad that Sandra, the chatterbox from yesterday, was nowhere to be seen.

"I don't see how that would make someone decide to murder him though," Dot said. "If they were annoyed about Thomas leaving the restaurant, killing him isn't going to get the veg chopped, is it?"

"It wouldn't be good timing for the restaurant though, would it?" Pea countered. "They got a Michelin star a couple of months ago and there's only three of them. If he's using the success to bail on them and get a better job, I can see them being annoyed."

Mary dabbed at her mouth in a manner that was far more lady like than the way she had just demolished the panini. "I can see someone maybe experiencing a flash of anger when they found out he was leaving," she said, "but not poisoning, that's got to be planned, surely? I mean, the kitchen is full of knives, a stabbing would make more sense for a flash of anger."

"Maybe they had something poisonous lying around and just decided to use it on the spur of the moment?" Pea shrugged.

"I hadn't thought of that," Mary said, cursing herself for not performing a more thorough search of the kitchen.

"The police looked at everything though," Dot said, "and after you had whispered sweet nothings into Inspector Corrigan's ear I wouldn't be surprised if he'd gone around and tasted everything himself."

"Haha," Mary said, her eyes daggers. She noticed

a man in a blue pin-stripe suit looking at her over Dot's shoulder. He was sitting at a table on the other side of the room, a newspaper in his hand and a coffee mug paused halfway to his lips. He was staring at Mary as though she had sprouted a new head, but she was used to it. Decades on prime time TV meant that your privacy was rarely your own. She ignored him and turned back to the others.

"There must be something about the timing," Pea said.

"What do you mean?"

"Well, why then?" he continued. "I mean if you were going to poison someone, does it make sense that you'd do it when there was a room full of people there?"

"Bloody hell Pea, you're a genius! You've got it!" Mary said, punching him on the arm in excitement and causing him to swear as he rubbed it. "That's exactly why they did it then!"

"You're going to have to explain that a bit," Dot said before sipping her tea, unmoved by Mary's excitement.

"Well," Mary began, but stopped as the light from the window which faced out onto the street was blocked by a figure. She turned to see the man who had been staring at her looking down with a nervous smile.

"Excuse me, but I couldn't help noticing you and..."

"No problem," Mary said wearily. "Do you want a picture or an autograph?"

"Oh!" The man exclaimed, taking a step backwards as though he had been stung. "No, no I wouldn't dream of bothering you on such a trivial manner when you are with friends!" He flashed the same nervous smile at Dot and Pea.

"Oh," Mary said, "then how can I help you?..."

He looked around the small café, before pulling out the spare chair at the table and landing in it heavily before leaning forward and talking in a low voice.

"Is it true that you were at the Rudolph hotel last night?"

Mary's eyes flickered to Dot and Pea, who were both looking just as bemused and surprised as she was.

"Yes," she answered slowly.

"I don't suppose you could tell me what happened exactly, could you?" the man asked, his voice awash with nervous excitement.

"Are you a reporter?"

"Oh! No! Nothing like that! I just have... a business interest."

"Look, tell us exactly who you are and why you

want to know or I'm calling the police right now," Mary said, leaning back in her chair and folding her arms as she fixed him with her hardest stare.

He was a plain and simple looking man with a face that was born to blend into a crowd. Mary was fairly sure that if she closed her eyes and he went and sat on another table, she would struggle to pick him out. He took a deep breath, exhaled slowly and nodded.

"Very well, I am Mr Sanker and I represent a group interested in the purchase of the Rudolph Hotel."

"You're the one who's been talking to Roderick Sutton?"

"That's right," he nodded encouragingly. "Everything seemed to be moving along swimmingly, but I'm afraid we've met some resistance from Mr Sutton's partner."

"Spencer Harley, he doesn't want to sell," Mary added.

"Quite so." The little man nodded.

"I'm still not entirely sure what this has to do with what happened last night?"

"Well," the man said, shifting awkwardly on his seat. "A sudden death like that, well..." he shrugged, "it can give a place a bit of a reputation."

"You mean you thought you could maybe get the

place cheaper if there was some juicy story in the papers about a death to put tourists off?" Dot said.

Mr Sanker gave a nervous laugh. "I realise that does sound a little crass, but you're quite right. I saw that Miss Blake here was going to be at the event tonight and guessed you had been there. When I saw you here today, I thought it would be a good chance to find out what happened and see if we could use it as leverage somehow."

"Then I tell you what," Mary said, "I'll tell you exactly what happened last night if you tell me everything about this deal to buy the hotel."

He frowned at her with a smile on his lips and then nodded.

"Very well. There isn't much to tell, though. My firm wishes to purchase the property and turn it into a number of flats. We had agreed on a fee with Mr Sutton and believed everything to be going well until there was a delay in getting the final signed paperwork back."

"Because Spencer Harley wouldn't sign it?"

"Correct. Mr Sutton had led us to believe that his partner was fully on board with the sale, but when we pressed him on getting the papers signed he confessed that Mr Harley was actually quite reluctant. I then visited Mr Harley and he told me he would only sell over his dead body."

"And yet you're still here trying to persuade him?"

"We have already put a substantial amount of money into the project. Architectural plans, lawyers, meeting with the town council," he trailed off shaking his head.

"I assume this offer is a decent one?" Mary said with one eyebrow raised.

"Oh! Very decent! The hotel really doesn't make any money and is in need of a great deal of repair. We feel the offer is in line with market value, but the truth is, on the open market they're very unlikely to find a buyer." He paused and smiled at Mary expectantly. "Now, if anything that occurred last night were to help things along, I would be very grateful."

Mary smiled sweetly at him as she stood up from the table. "I'm sorry, but Spencer Harley is a friend so I couldn't possibly betray his confidence."

"But... but you said!" the man blustered, rising to his feet to face her.

"I'm an actress," Mary replied with a shrug, "I've been lying for a living for almost thirty years." She turned and strode out from the café, hoping that Pea and Dot were following her and that Mr Sanker wasn't.

CHAPTER FOURTEEN

"You shouldn't wind people up like that, Mary," Pea said as he and Dot caught up with her brisk walk along the High Street. "That man could be the murderer for all you know!"

"What? Of course, he isn't!"

"How do you know?! Think about it. He's desperate for this sale to go through, right? And Spencer had said only over his dead body?"

"Yes," Dot interrupted, "but there's a bit of a flaw in that theory, isn't there? Spencer wasn't the one who died."

"Well, no," Pea admitted, "but maybe he was the target."

Mary stopped walking and turned to him. "What do you mean?"

"We've been thinking that someone meant to kill Thomas, but what if they were trying to kill someone else at dinner?"

"You mean they could have been after Spencer?"

"Or anyone!" he answered, throwing his hands up in the air. "That's if it was poison at all, of course..."

"It was," Mary snapped back. "But you make a good point. We should try and find out what was going on with all of them. Maybe Spencer was in the way of the hotel sale, but there could be other things going on."

"What are you thinking?" Dot asked. She had known Mary long enough to know when an idea was brewing.

"Before we were interrupted in the café, Pea said something that got me thinking."

"Oh yes!" Pea said with a broad grin. "You said I was a genius if I recall?"

Mary shook her head. "No... that doesn't sound like something I'd say. Anyway, you were wondering why on earth someone would try and murder someone with all those people there as witnesses, but maybe that was the whole point? Maybe they wanted all those people there so that there were lots of suspects?"

"But why would any of the others be suspects? What reason did any of them have for killing Thomas?" Dot said.

"Well, we know that he was planning on leaving the restaurant, maybe that was something to do with it? And then there's always the crime of passion," she smirked.

"Surprise, surprise," Dot said rolling her eyes. "Mary thinks sex has got something to do with it."

"Oh, come on," Pea grumbled, his face wrinkled in disgust, "that's my sister,"

"I'm not talking about sex," Mary snapped, "I'm talking about unrequited love." She smiled as she watched their faces react with sudden interest. "I noticed at breakfast that James Donovan seems to have a thing for Daisy, but when I asked her about it she seemed angry."

"Well, if I was James, it wouldn't be Daisy I was after. It would be Ruth."

"I beg your pardon?" Dot snapped.

"Oh, well it's not big news," Pea said with a shrug, "I'd imagine half the men in town have a thing for that girl."

Mary noticed Dot shoot him an angry sideways glance.

"Bloody hell Pea," Mary said, mostly because

Dot's reaction seemed to warrant it "She's half your age! Anyway, that was pretty much my point. Thomas was a good-looking young man, he and Ruth worked together, maybe there was something there?"

"But what has that got to do with James and Daisy?" Dot asked.

"Who knows? But there could have been some sort of love triangle going on. Maybe Daisy is angry with him because he was after Ruth as well?"

"And so you think the bartender, James, might have bumped Thomas off to clear the field?" Dot chipped in.

"Exactly!" Mary said, her mind racing with possibilities. "And then there's Anna Crosby."

"What would she want to murder Thomas for?" Pea asked.

"Well, she doesn't seem to be the most stable person and I think she likes a drink a bit too much. There was something odd about the way Ruth was protecting her, maybe Thomas had some dirt on her he was going to expose?"

"This is all well and good," Dot said haughtily. "But there's no point in just making up all these things, we need to talk to them and find out what's really going on."

"Of course, but at least this gives us a starting

point. I suggest we split up, each tackle someone different."

"You're beginning to sound like a professional outfit," a voice said from behind her. She turned to see Inspector Joe Corrigan, his dark brown eyes twinkling mischievously under his mop of brown hair. "That is," he continued, "apart from discussing a potential murder case in the middle of the street."

"Maybe if people weren't eavesdropping into private conversations it wouldn't be an issue?" Mary said, raising her chin defiantly. "Have you managed to do your job and find out how he was poisoned yet?"

Mary felt Dot and Pea edge away, as though they sensed this was something between Mary and Corrigan and not them.

The Inspector's smile faded, his face turning serious, business like.

"He wasn't poisoned, Mary. I got the lab to test everything he ate, there was no poison in anything."

"And what about the post-mortem?" Mary asked. "Do they know why he died?"

"It hasn't been done yet." He shrugged. "There's paperwork, lack of resources... Look, Mary, I rushed the tests on the food through because you seemed so certain something was wrong here, but there was nothing. If he was poisoned, it would have had to have been in the food, you all shared from the same wine bottles and coffee pots. "I'm sorry, but I think the post-mortem will show that Thomas Moseley died from his underlying heart condition."

Mary stared back at him, her face like cold marble. Why did she feel that this was so wrong? If Thomas had died from natural causes, then it was a tragic, but unavoidable event. Surely that was preferable to murder? That someone should deliberately try and cut that young life short? So why was she so sure? She pictured his face again, twisted in pain, confusion and anguish. As she did so she felt the now familiar pang deep in her gut that something was terribly, terribly wrong. She might not be able to explain it, but she knew she was right.

"No," she said quietly, "I'm sorry, but you're wrong. That man was murdered, I'm sure of it, and I'm not going to leave this alone until I've proved it."

Corrigan took a deep breath, his lips tightening as his deep brown eyes stared back at the defiance in her eyes.

"Just be careful, Mary. People don't take kindly to being accused of murder, especially when there's no evidence." He waited a moment, but when Mary didn't respond, he continued. "And think of his parents, think how upsetting this could be for them if they hear that someone is claiming foul play?"

Mary closed her eyes and took a deep breath. She was experiencing something that she rarely had during her life. She was embarrassed. She felt like a foolish little girl who had been playing at a game she didn't understand and was now being admonished by the adults. There was a sense of loss there as well. She could feel the enormity of her acting career being over, threatening to rise up from the depths where she had buried it. Why had she wanted this so much? Why had she felt the need to pull at threads, to poke into corners? Was it just to give herself a sense of purpose, to prove to herself and the world that she wasn't past it?

"No," she said suddenly, feeling her rush of emotions cool into something hard, like steel. "I'm doing this because I looked into a young man's eyes and I saw how afraid he was, and how confused. Then I sat with him as he died and I know that something was not right about it." She knew she was saying it as much for herself as for Corrigan, but she no longer cared. She folded her arms and stared into the deep brown eyes of the inspector. "Let me know what happens at the autopsy. Until then, I'll just continue to do your job here."

She turned and marched off down the street without looking back. Dot, who had stayed a few yards away with Pea, followed. Pea gave a quick, awkward smile at the inspector before he scampered after them.

Corrigan watched them go and raised one hand to his chin thoughtfully as a smile crept across his lips.

CHAPTER FIFTEEN

"I'm fairly sure this could be considered stalking," Dot said, her mouth pursed in disapproval.

"Oh, don't be so melodramatic," Mary answered without a hint of irony. "I just fancied a gin and tonic that's all."

"Yes," Dot said in a flat voice. "It's just funny how you suddenly fancied one after you saw James Donovan come in here, isn't it?"

Mary rolled her eyes and scanned the room.

Dot was right. As Mary had been storming back to the hotel, unable to even speak to Dot and Pea in her fury, she had suddenly seen the young barman from the hotel entering a pub set back from the High street. She had immediately declared her raking thirst, causing Dot's eyebrows to become almost permanently raised in suspicion.

James was playing darts with a couple of lads his age, laughing and joking as though he didn't have a care in the world. Was this normal behaviour after someone you knew had so recently died? Mary thought back to her youth and admonished herself. Of course it was, the young had a remarkable propensity to bouncing back.

"So now we're here definitely not stalking him," Pea said sarcastically, "what exactly is the plan?"

"Well, I think we should ask him what he was talking about with Edward Landry, don't you?" Mary shrugged. "The two of them clearly think someone might have done it, so why haven't they told the police?"

"And you think he's just going to tell you?" Dot asked cynically.

"Well," Mary said draining the last of her gin and tonic which she had finished at breakneck speed, "there's only one way to find out."

She stood up and walked along the bar towards the dartboard at the back. James was taking his shot, but she watched the gaze of the other two men notice her and stare with widening eyes.

"James?" she said in what she considered her most sultry voice.

"Miss Blake?" he said, turning around from collecting his darts in bewilderment.

She looked between his two friends who were stood either side of him and both grinning from ear to ear.

"I was wondering if I could buy you a drink?" Mary said, putting her hands on her hips and shifting them to one side in what she hoped would still pass as an attractive manner.

"Erm..." James said, looking pale and confused.

"James!" hissed the man on the left, "Go on you bloody idiot!"

"Right, yes," James stammered, handing the darts to the hisser before stepping towards her.

She turned and moved towards the bar, her eyes searching across the room until she saw Pea and Dot, who had obviously swapped chairs to watch the show. Pea was grinning as Dot shook head slowly in despair.

Internally, Mary was feeling rather pleased. She had kept herself in shape and although she was facing a now constant battle with sagging flesh and skin, she still clearly had enough about her to impress. Although it could be that men of around twenty weren't exactly choosy when it came to a chance with the opposite sex.

"What can I get you, James?" she asked, hopping onto one of the tatty leather stools as she reached the bar.

"Erm, I'll have a lager top please."

She ordered it along with another gin and tonic for her and watched as he gulped at the frothy pint nervously.

"Have you worked at the hotel long?"

"A couple of years," he said shrugging. "It's alright, I don't have to do much."

"That's good," Mary answered with a smile. "It must have been a shock to you, Thomas dying?"

He looked at her, frowning. "Yeah," he answered, but his voice sounded different, warier.

Mary realised he was already suspicious of her motives. No matter how much she tried to charm information out of him, the likelihood of a fifty-year-old TV actress coming on to a hotel bartender in his early twenties had obviously occurred to him. Time to take another tack.

"Look, James," she said, leaning towards him. "I know you think there might have been something more to Thomas's death than just his heart condition."

"What do you mean?" he said, his thin cheeks flushing red.

"My friends heard you talking to the hotel manager, Edward Landry. It sounded as though you thought a woman might have done something to Thomas?"

His mouth opened and closed like a fish as his expression ranged from confusion to fear.

"I was just being stupid," he said shaking his head. "The whole thing just messed me up and I was a bit all over the place, I didn't know what I was saying."

"Sometimes our first reaction can be more on the nose than we think," Mary said in a calming voice.

He frowned at her. "Do you know something? Did Anna say something to you?"

Mary tried not to show any reaction to the mention of the head chef's name. "She told me some things. About Thomas, yes," she lied.

"Look," he said, leaning forward himself now, his voice lowered conspiratorially, "I know what you're thinking, I thought the same thing, but it doesn't make sense if you really go through it properly."

"Why not?" Mary asked, playing along despite being now hopelessly lost in the conversation.

"Well everyone in the kitchen knew that if Thomas left the restaurant was done for, and I thought the same as you, maybe Anna did something to him." He shook his head and looked down at his drink. "She was definitely desperate enough. But then that wouldn't make sense, would it?"

"Why not?"

"Because then he'd be gone anyway! Anna would

still have the same problem of barely being able to boil an egg!"

Mary tried to keep her face impassive despite the rush of excitement which was racing through her. "So Anna killing him wouldn't have solved her problems anyway?" she said, in what she hoped was a level voice.

"Of course not!" he said, waving his free hand dismissively before pausing and looking at her curiously. "Do you think Thomas was killed then? Have you heard something from the police?"

"All I know is they are still looking into it," Mary said in a tone that suggested foul play more certainly than if she had said it out loud. She felt no guilt at this slight deception. After all, the autopsy was still to be done and if she was right, the police would be back on the case soon enough.

"Bloody hell," James said taking another large swig of his beer.

"Can you think of anyone other than Anna that would have wanted Thomas out of the way?"

He gave a hollow laugh. "The restaurant going under wasn't exactly good news for any of us, it was pretty much propping the hotel up."

"So anyone could have had a reason for taking it out on Thomas?"

"No!" he cried suddenly. "Look, we were all

pretty pissed off when Thomas said he was leaving, but you couldn't really blame him. He was getting a crap deal and everyone knew he was going to go on to be some big-shot chef somewhere. No one would have bloody killed him because of it."

It was Mary's turn to look thoughtfully at her drink.

"Except Roderick, I guess," James said.

"Roderick?"

"Well, everyone knows he wants to sell the place, now that Thomas has gone it is more or less going to be a done deal."

"And did he know about Thomas leaving?" Mary asked urgently, her heart racing.

"Oh no, Anna and Ruth only knew a few days ago and Edward and I only found out yesterday morning. I told Daisy and she was so upset, cried her eyes out, she did."

"Are you two an item?" Mary asked, wondering if she'd get a different reaction than when she had asked Daisy.

"She's a lovely girl," James said, blushing.

"Thank you, James, I'll see you later," Mary said, jumping from her stool and gesturing for the others to follow her out of the pub and back onto the streets of Parchester.

CHAPTER SIXTEEN

"You are joking?" Pea said, incredulous.

"Nope, according to James, Anna Crosby can't even boil an egg."

"But how is that possible? She's got a Michelin star!"

"The restaurant has," Mary corrected him. "What if Thomas Mosley was the real talent in the kitchen? What if he was the one that was actually running the show?"

"But then how did Anna become a head chef?"

"That's exactly what I want to ask Spencer," Mary said in an annoyed tone. "I knew he was keeping things from us, but to not mention something like this!" She watched Dot and Pea exchange glances in front of her. "You two can knock that off as well!" She snapped.

She knew she was angrier than they thought she should be, but she felt totally justified in the hot temper that was coursing through her. Spencer Harley had invited her here because he was being blackmailed, but had then refused to show her the blackmail letters or share with her any information that would even remotely help her find who was behind them until after Thomas's death where he then announces he thinks it might have been his business partner all along! Now she finds out that the head chef he was so fond of, is a fraud. As far as she was concerned, this was the straw that broke the camel's back.

She called Spencer's mobile as she marched back down the street towards the café that they were soon going to be considered regulars at if they kept this up.

"Mary?" he answered in a somewhat weary tone of voice.

"Yes, get to the Tumbledown Café on the High street now, we've got things to discuss." She hung up before he could reply and entered the café.

"Oh! Back again, are we?" Sandra cooed from behind the counter.

"For the third time actually," Mary smiled. The woman's round and pleasant face disarming her anger almost immediately. She just hoped she wasn't going to chew her ear off again.

They chatted as she ordered drinks for her, Dot and Pea before the three of them took their seats in the same corner they had sat in earlier.

Their conversation was stilted as Mary sulked in thought and the others, wary of her earlier outburst, stayed quiet and sipped their coffee. It was roughly ten minutes later when the small bell tinkled over the café door and Mary looked up to see a red-faced Spencer, flat cap in hand, his small, round eyes scanning the room. They landed on Mary and he gave a small nod before ordering a coffee at the counter and moving across to join them.

"Hello all," he said as he heaved himself onto the small wooden chair that was vacant.

"Don't you hello me!" Mary said, her anger suddenly rising back to her immediately. "Just when were you planning on telling us the truth about any of this?!"

Spencer frowned at her before looking to Dot and Pea for support. They carefully kept their expressions blank, and finding no comfort there, he turned back to Mary.

"I'm sorry Mary, I'm not sure what you mean?"

"Not sure what I mean?!" Mary laughed mirthlessly. "First you get us down here on some rubbish about blackmail, then you casually announce that you knew who was doing it all along, and now we find out that the only person who's keeping the hotel afloat is a fraud!"

Spencer blinked. "A fraud? I'm sorry, who are you talking about?"

"Anna Crosby of course!"

Spencer recoiled as though he had been slapped. "Anna? What on earth are you talking about?!"

There was a pause as a young and disinterested looking waitress arrived with Spencer's coffee before Mary picked up her thread again, now with a slightly calmer tone.

"I mean, that your precious chef is apparently no more a cook than I am!"

"I don't... I don't understand," stammered Spencer, now looking around the group in confusion.

"She means," Dot said, deciding that the conversation wasn't getting very far, "that we've heard Anna is just the figurehead in the kitchen, but that Thomas was the real talent."

Spencer's rotund face slowly changed from furrowed brow to a wide smile as he began to chuckle. "Ridiculous!" he said shaking his head. "Thomas was just a boy. You can't compare him with the expertise of Anna! I don't know who's been telling you this nonsense, but that's exactly what it is, nonsense."

"Where was Anna working before you hired her for the restaurant?" Mary asked softly.

"Where was she working?" Spencer said, his expression changing curiously. "What has that go to do with anything?"

"I was just wondering what her reputation was like before you employed her?"

"Well, I've known her for a number of years..." his voice trailed off as one chubby hand reached out to begin fiddling with the salt pot which sat on the table in front of him.

"How did you know her?" Mary asked, deciding on attempting a new angle to attack this sudden reluctance to talk.

Spencer snorted in annoyance. "If you must know, Anna was my secretary."

Mary's mouth fell open somewhat in surprise. She glanced at Dot and Pea, who were both sporting similar looks of surprise and confusion.

"She was your secretary?"

"Yes, that's right. What of it?"

"I'm sorry," Mary continued, "I don't understand. How did she go from being your secretary to being head chef at the restaurant?"

"She'd always had ambitions towards being a chef and I could tell she had talent, nothing more.

The opportunity at the hotel came up and I encouraged her to take it."

"So she didn't have any experience of running a restaurant before, or even working in one?"

"No, but she was a very competent secretary and she brought me in odd things she had cooked and they were always very lovely." He said this defiantly, his chin raised as if defying them to question the decision. "In any case, it was the right choice, the success of the restaurant proves it."

"Unless that success was down to her staff members rather than her?" Mary said.

Spencer looked up at her sharply. "Even if it was the case that she delegated well, she still runs the kitchen, the success is hers. Now look here, I called you into this thinking you would be a discreet way of proving that Roderick was trying to blackmail me into selling the hotel. That doesn't mean to say I want you muck-raking all sorts of nonsense with the hotel staff and claiming murder when a man has died a perfectly natural death! I think it's best for all concerned that you leave the hotel as soon as possible." He stood up and strode purposefully from the café, leaving his coffee untouched on the table.

CHAPTER SEVENTEEN

"It still doesn't make sense to me that Anna would do anything to hurt Thomas," Dot said as they walked back to the hotel. "It doesn't help her run the restaurant now, does it? If he really was the talent behind their success, it's not exactly going to be able to maintain standards now he's dead."

"Everyone keeps saying that, but who knows what people might do when the red mist descends. We need to talk to Ruth Faulkner," Mary said decisively. "If Thomas was the one really running the kitchen, then Ruth would know and she might be more likely to admit it than Anna. I can't believe I didn't notice something going on this morning!"

"What do you mean?" Pea asked as he neatly sidestepped an old lady who whizzed past on a mobility scooter at a rate of knots.

"Can you remember what Anna said at breakfast when she ran out of the room? She said she, 'couldn't just replace him' and that it was 'all over now'. At the time I thought she was just being emotional about losing a colleague, but now we know what we know, it all sounds very different. Then, when I talked to her and Ruth in the kitchen, there was something off about their relationship."

"You mean, they were..." Dot paused, searching for the words. "Romantically involved?"

"Bloody hell Dot," Mary said, laughing at her awkwardness, "sometimes I think you've been thawed out from the nineteenth century, but the answer is no, I don't mean they were 'romantically involved'." She said this last part in a mockingly serious tone before becoming more thoughtful. "It was odd, it was as though the relationship was the other way around from how I imagined it."

"How do you mean?" Pea asked as they came to a stop outside the doors of the hotel.

"Well you know the reputation chefs have, all swearing and bossing people about and things, but Anna doesn't seem like that at all. In fact, it was like Ruth was a concerned parent or something."

Pea sighed and looked up at the hotel next to them. "This also explains why breakfast was not up to scratch."

"Not that it seemed to slow you down any," Dot said raising an eyebrow at him. "So what's the plan now?"

"This has got to be centred on the kitchen," Mary said. "That's where Thomas worked, that's where he was planning to quit and leave them high and dry, and it's also where he was killed. The answer has to be there somewhere."

"Right," Pea said clapping his hands together, "I'm about ready to eat again, so the restaurant works for me!"

Dot and Mary rolled their eyes simultaneously as the three of them headed inside.

As soon as they had climbed the short steps and entered through the wide, old doors of the Rudolph Hotel, Mary heard her name being called from across the high-ceilinged lobby.

"Mary! Just the lady I wanted to talk to!" She turned to her right where Roderick Sutton was halfway through the door to the bar area when he had clearly turned and spotted her entering.

Mary looked at the others who had halted on the smooth wood floor. "You two go on and I'll catch you up."

Dot frowned but turned away towards the direction of the restaurant after Pea, who had already set off at pace.

"Roderick," Mary said, forcing a smile to her face. "How can I help?"

"Come on through," Roderick said, holding the bar door open. "We'll have to serve our own drinks I'm afraid as everything's shut, but I pour better measures in any case." He gave her a wink as she passed while he held the door open and she felt a small quiver of repulsion.

Roderick Sutton wasn't an ugly man. Despite his rather large Roman nose, which stuck out of his narrow face like a shark fin, his high cheekbones and dark eyes had a certain handsomeness to them. For Mary, though, there was something inherently unlikeable about the man, something creepy. She had thought so on first being introduced to him and now, having heard how Spencer talked of him, the feeling had only hardened. He had the look of a smooth operator, or more accurately, someone who thought they were. He was in his late thirties but had a kind of boyish nature that made even these modest years seem too many. His loose quiff of dark hair flopped around on his headband and required constant pulling back into place with his long fingers, something that seemed to Mary almost an unconscious habit.

He moved swiftly behind the bar and began making gin and tonics for both of them.

"I know you like a G & T, saw you have one the other day. I'm quite partial myself."

Mary took a seat on one of the padded bar stools. "What was it you wanted to talk to me about?" she asked, keen to get to the point so she could extradite herself from here and get to the restaurant.

"What do you make of Parchester?" Roderick asked, completely ignoring her.

"It seems like a pretty little town," Mary answered. Now she thought about it, she had barely given any thought to her surroundings since she had arrived. She made a mental note to correct this in future. Who knows what information you might glean from observing a place closely?

She surprised herself by suddenly feeling guilty and ashamed at the realisation she was trying to think like a detective. Was there some part of her brain that was planning to take on future cases?

"It's pretty enough," Roderick said as he slid her G&T across the bar to her, "but it suffers from a lack of ambition."

"Can a town have ambition?"

"Well it should have if it knows what's good for it," Roderick laughed as he leaned forward and planted his elbows on the polished wood of the bar next to her. "These places are always little bustling things full of small businesses and gossip until the corporations turn up. Once there's a big new shopping centre on the outskirts of town, things will look pretty different here."

"Maybe not for the better," Mary said, eyebrows raised.

Roderick laughed again. "Of course it will be for the better! More jobs, more money sloshing around the place. Instead of the young people of the town leaving for the city to find work, they can stay here, enjoy the scenery and still earn decent money."

Mary sensed there was something else at play here, that Roderick was merely doing the groundwork before getting to the reason he had wanted to speak to her. "You're talking about this as if it's going to happen?" She asked innocently.

His eyes sparkled as one corner of his mouth rose in a smile. "You're an intelligent woman, Miss Blake. Yes, I have been privy to plans that might change things around here."

"And let me guess," Mary said, the penny finally dropping, somehow this is tied up with you wanting to sell the hotel?"

He smiled, looked down at his drink and swirled it making the ice cubes clink. "Spencer is a bit of an old romantic," he said, "he gets attached to things and it means he can't see things clearly."

"How did you and he end up partners in this?"

Mary asked, it only just occurring to her what odd bedfellows they were.

"He's an old friend of the family," Roderick answered lightly. He looked at her with a grin. "As you'll know with your background, people from 'old money' stick together."

"So your family encouraged Spencer to work with you?"

"No family left," he said in a hollow voice, the smile vanishing from his lips. "Just me left with the small amount of money left in the coffers after my father drank most of it and my mother faded away like a ghost."

"I'm sorry," Mary said.

"Oh, don't be," Roderick said with a wave of his glass, the smile returning. "I've had more than most in life, but I don't plan to sit around and turn into Spencer, rattling around in some dusty old house while pining for some unrequited love."

"You mean Anna Crosby?"

His face jerked back slightly in surprise. "You do pay attention, don't you? Yes, Spencer's besotted with the woman, lord knows why though, she's as timid as a mouse."

Mary took a long sip of her drink, her brain working overtime as it sifted through these bits of information. Well, this was no time to pussy-foot around. "What do you make of Anna's cooking skills?"

Roderick laughed, his head leaning back and his great nose pointing to the ceiling. "You know?" he said when he had calmed slightly, "you're far more like your on-screen character than I ever thought! So you know the hotel's dirty little secret, do you? Anna Crosby can't cook to save her life. Truth be told, I'm not exactly sure what Anna can do."

"And yet you hired her to be head chef in the hotel kitchen?"

"Well, Spencer did obviously. I only found out this morning when Edward told me. He's in a flap because without Thomas the restaurant might as well pack up now."

"Even if you didn't know at the time, you must have known it was a big risk making his receptionist your head chef?"

"Look," he said, draining the last of his drink, "this place was only meant to be a short-term investment, Spencer knew that. When we bought it the place was already failing, we got it cheap so the previous owners could clear off their debts in a hurry."

"And the plan was to sell it on to developers?" Mary asked.

"Exactly, but they weren't quite ready to play

ball, building permits etc," he waved his hand dismissively. "So we decided to keep the place running in the hope we could at least cover our loan payments on the place. Spencer brought Anna in and by some miracle, or curse, it worked. Now I find out it's because we ended up with Thomas Mosley."

"Why a curse? You lucked out with Thomas, didn't you? The restaurant is making money."

"Well, that's just the problem, isn't it? When Spencer told me he wanted to hire Anna to run the place, someone with no experience, I couldn't see the harm. We'd make a few quid just because of the lack of competition in town, if nothing else. When the place started to get rave reviews and was booked out for weeks on end I couldn't believe it, which was when I discovered it was Thomas running the kitchen. Half the time Anna was just sat in the back with a bottle of wine."

"Still, that would only make the place more valuable, wouldn't it?"

"Not to investors. They don't care about the restaurant or the hotel, they want to rip the guts of it out and turn it into flats. The problem was the local planning committee. They were starting to get cold feet about giving permission for the change of use." He stood up and took a deep breath. "Look, this place has had it. Either we sell up, or Spencer is going to lose a lot of money as well as me. He called you down here for the opening, he must trust you. Maybe you could talk to him?"

Mary gave a small laugh. So now they had reached the reason why he had really wanted to talk to her.

"You want me to pressure Spencer into selling the hotel?"

"Not pressure," he shrugged, "just talk it through with him."

Mary finished her own drink. "It occurs to me, that you would have had a very good reason for getting Thomas Mosley out of the way."

Roderick's calm and somewhat arrogant composure seemed to vanish instantly. His face paled. "What are you talking about? I wouldn't have wanted that to happen, no matter what! Thomas was a good chap!"

"Still, it's convenient for you that the restaurant will now be on the slide isn't it?"

"I don't understand your point," he said, his poise and features now recovered and looking more angry by the second. "Thomas had a heart condition, it was just one of those things."

"I'm not so sure," Mary said, standing, "but I'm going to find out." She turned and left without looking back.

CHAPTER EIGHTEEN

Mary wasn't sure what Roderick would make of their brief conversation, but she had learnt something from dealing with the press for all of those years. Often it was better to leave something hanging and walk away than to get down into the nitty-gritty of it. If you'd used a juicy enough worm, the bait would be taken in due course.

As she opened the door to the restaurant, she could tell she had missed something interesting. Dot and Pea were sat at one of the tables to her right with Anna Crosby. The three of them had looked up at her as though a gunshot rang out. Anna's eyes were wide and wet with tears.

"It's ok," Dot said, patting Anna's hand which she held in her hers across the table. "It's just Mary."

Mary made her way over and sat down as Anna's eyes sank to the white tablecloth. She looked at Pea who made a face that she recognised from her childhood as the same one he made when her parents were arguing. It roughly translated as, 'Blimey, someone here may be unhinged'.

"How are you, Anna?" she said turning to her. After a moment's pause, Dot replied for the chef instead.

"Anna's just been telling us about what's been going on in the restaurant since she came here." She turned to the downcast eyes of the chef. "Why don't you go over it again, Anna? It will help to get it all out, won't it?"

Anna gave an unsure smile but began talking in a quiet voice.

"I'd always wanted to be a cook," she began, "and then when Spencer said there was a restaurant here that they wanted to revamp, I just couldn't believe it. I thought this would be my chance to get into it all, start learning the trade."

Mary shot a glance at Dot and Pea. Learning the trade?!

"When Spencer said I was going to be head chef, I... I didn't know what to do. I didn't want to let him down, but I didn't have a clue what I was doing!

Thank goodness Thomas came along." She paused, a flash of pain crossing her face as she picked up the already wet tissue in front of her and blew her nose loudly.

"Tell me about Thomas," Mary continued in a soothing voice.

"Oh." Anna gave a small laugh and shook her head. "He was so amazing. He came in for an interview and instead of persuading us to give him a chance he just cooked us the most incredible breakfast." I hired him right there on the spot, and Ruth the next day. They were such a good team. Ruth is so enthusiastic, always wearing a smile. She did all the grunt work while Thomas organised the menus and ordered the ingredients and things. It was only a couple of weeks until I realised I wasn't needed any more. I chopped the veg, prepped some things, and Thomas taught me things along the way." She looked down suddenly and sobbed.

"What is it?" Mary asked, sensing there was something more than just the death of her young colleague there.

"I took all the glory," she said in a sob. I was the one getting my picture in the paper, I was the one getting the praise for a Michelin star. I wanted to tell everyone, but I knew that if I did it would all be over and I would be letting Spencer down. He'd trusted me, put himself on the line to give me this chance." Her voice faded as the tissue fought a losing battle against the streaming tears and nose.

"And you knew Thomas was going to leave?" Mary asked.

Anna nodded. "Yes, he'd told Ruth and I. I couldn't blame him, who would want to stay on here in this situation?" She waved her hand around to gesture at the restaurant.

Mary frowned. None of this was quite what she had been expecting. In her mind, Anna had been the one who had stood to lose the most with Thomas leaving. The sham of her reputation would be exposed, her career would effectively be over. She would have let Spencer down as the restaurant began to lose the reputation it had built. Yet the woman before them, looking meekly down at the table and snuffling into a tissue, didn't seem capable of raising her voice in anger, let alone murder.

"How did Ruth react to the news that Thomas was leaving?"

"Oh, nothing ever seems to bother Ruth very much. She always seems to have some other plan to bounce her back."

As if her words had conjured her remaining colleague from thin air, Ruth Faulkner appeared from the kitchen door carrying a tray that contained two large coffee pots, a number of cups, and a plate full of mints that were clearly designed to be given out with a bill.

"Do I hear my ears burning?" Ruth said with a slight smile.

"I was just saying how you're always so positive," Anna said, squeezing the young woman's hand affectionately as she laid down the tray.

"Oh, there's no point in letting things drag you down," she said as she began passing out cups.

"Not even if a colleague dies suddenly?" Mary asked.

Ruth paused, her hand halfway to delivering a cup to Pea. "Oh, well obviously there are some things you can't help but be affected by," she answered in a quiet voice. There was a period where the only sound in the high ceilinged restaurant was the clink of spoons on grocery and quietly muttered 'thank you's' for passing the milk.

"Were you and Thomas close?" Mary said, blowing across the top of her steaming mug.

"Thomas was a good bloke," Ruth answered, in what Mary thought was a side-step of her question. "But he was very focused on his work. He didn't have much time for anything else, really."

There was a moment of silence as the occupants

of the table reflected on the death of the young cook.

"Do you both plan to stay on here?" Pea said, attempting to move the conversation on.

Anna gave a humourless laugh. "I think my days of playing chef are over," she said with a sigh. "Ruth here is going to write a book though, aren't you Ruth?"

"Um, yes," Ruth said in what seemed to be a rare instance of shyness.

"Oh!" Pea said with a broad smile. "What's it going to be about?"

"It's a recipe book actually," Ruth answered.

"Oh right, well that's great, well done." Pea nodded back at her, beaming.

"Thank you." Ruth smiled sweetly. "I better be getting home," she said rising. I'll call you later, Anna?" She squeezed her boss's shoulder and Anna patted her hand.

"Yes, thank you."

Ruth gave a quick goodbye to everyone, turned on her heels and left the restaurant.

"Was it something I said?" Pea said, joking at her quick exit.

Something in the phrase struck a chord with Mary, though.

"Ruth's cookbook," she said, turning to Anna, "is she using some of Thomas's recipes, do you know?"

Anna looked startled. "Oh, I don't know. I'm sure Ruth has come up with her own, though."

"Yes, I'm sure," Mary said thoughtfully. "Did you know that there were plans to sell the hotel?"

"Oh yes, I remember Daisy being quite upset about it. Her father worked here for years, you know? I think she sees it as her home."

"And you weren't worried?"

She shook her head and smiled. "No, Spencer told me he wasn't going to sell the place. He loves it here." She gave a small laugh. "He really is very sweet."

Mary sat back in her seat as Anna, Pea and Dot continued the conversation without her. Ruth's cookbook had intrigued her. If Thomas really had been the genius cook they all thought he was, then his recipes could be worth something. Had Ruth decided to profit from her colleague's work? If so, maybe Thomas had found out and Ruth had decided to silence him. It sounded far-fetched even as she ran it through her own mind, but then nothing about the death of the young chef seemed real or justifiable at the moment. The contorted vision of his face seemed to flash in front of her as it had done a number of times since his death.

"Don't you think so, Mary?"

She looked up in confusion to the three faces around the table stared back at her.

"I'm sorry, what?"

"I said," Dot continued, "Don't you think it's interesting that Thomas had had an argument with James Donovan?"

"Oh, yes," Mary said vaguely, "interesting."

"Anyway," Anna said with a sigh, "I better go, I'm meeting Spencer."

"Where are you meeting him?" Mary asked, wondering if she should gate crash and ask more questions.

Anna gave a small smile as she rose, her cheeks flushing.

"We're going to Bella's in town," she said sheepishly. "I'll see you later." She turned and hurried away.

"We passed Bella's when we were in town," Pea said with a grin. "A little Italian place looked very romantic."

"Oh stop wiggling your eyebrows," Dot said sharply. "You're like a giggling schoolboy.

"What was that about an argument between James Donovan and Thomas?" Mary asked.

"I didn't think you were listening," Dot said with a questioning gaze. Mary answered it with silence before Pea broke in.

"More than just an argument...you saw James's black eye."

"That was from Thomas?" Mary exclaimed, leaning forward with interest.

"Yep, sounds like there was a bit of a love triangle. Did you really not hear any of that?!"

"No! Stop being astounded that I drifted off for a minute and just tell me!"

"Alright, alright!" Pea said, raising his hands in front of him defensively. "Anna was telling us that everyone seemed to be in love with Ruth, can't say I blame them, I mean she is quite the looker."

Dot hit him hard on the arm. "You're old enough to be her father!"

"Don't worry," Pea said grinning as he rubbed his arm, "I wasn't planning on making a move."

Dot adjusted herself in her seat hurriedly. "Yes, well perhaps I'd better explain if you can't be sensible."

Mary frowned at them both, thrown by this odd exchange, but before she could process what it meant Dot had continued talking.

"Anna said that Thomas had been smitten with Ruth and apparently she liked to lead him on."

"Lead him on? So she wasn't actually interested?"

Dot pursed her lips. "Seems the sort that would

enjoy leading people on more than actually having a relationship with them to me."

Mary frowned again. Was Dot now becoming an expert at reading people? In Mary's view, she had always seemed to see other people as some sort of alien species. Maybe she was softening? Or maybe she just had a bee in her bonnet over Ruth Faulkner after Pea's comments about the young woman earlier?

"Maybe she was leading him on in order to get recipes out of him for her book?" Pea said.

"Blimey," Mary said exhaling, "so what about James Donavon?"

"Anna thinks he was sweet on Ruth as well," Dot continued, "and that's why they had a bust-up. Thomas gave him the black eye he's got, whatever it was about."

Mary gave a slight smile at being 'sweet on someone'. Sometimes talking to Dot was like a portal to the 1950s.

"Well, I think we should ask him." Her phone buzzed in her pocket and she pulled it from her jeans. "Hello?"

"Mary, it's Inspector Corrigan," there was a slight pause, "Joe."

Mary felt a prickle of heat run up the back of her neck. "Hi Joe, any news on the autopsy?"

She heard him sigh down the phone, the small speaker at her ear crackling. "They didn't find anything conclusive, Mary."

"Conclusive? So, they did find something?"

"Not really, the doc says that he was generally in good health. He looked at his medical records and it looked as though his medication had his heart condition under control."

"So he thinks he might have been poisoned?"

"Well, the initial blood results didn't turn up anything out of the ordinary. If he was poisoned, we might never know unless we have an idea what to look for."

"So you need me to look into it and see if I can give you something to go on," she said thoughtfully.

"No, that's not what I said," he answered, sounding exasperated. "I want you to go home and try to forget about it. I can't investigate any more, there's nothing here to show that something suspicious happened."

Now the prickle of heat that ran up her neck and caused her face to flush was not from the sudden intimacy of Corrigan using his first name, it was from anger. He didn't believe her that there was something suspicious about the death of Thomas Mosley, he didn't trust her.

"Well, Inspector Corrigan, luckily you don't get

to decide what I do. I suggest you go back to chasing people who haven't paid their parking fines or whatever it is you have to do that is so much more important than a murder." She hung up the phone and dropped it onto the table in front of her.

She stared at it a moment before raising her head, intending to tell Pea and Dot the bad news, and that maybe she had had them barking up the wrong tree all along when a woman's scream rang out from the direction of the kitchen.

The three of them darted from their table and sprinted towards the swing door which led through to the kitchen. Mary reached it first and pushed it open to see Ruth crouched on the floor next to Spencer Harley who was twitching on the cold stone tiles.

"I don't know what's wrong with him!" Ruth cried, looking up at them, her eyes wide with fear and wet with tears. Mary bent down next to her and looked at Spencer's face, which shone with a waxy look under the strip lights of the kitchen. He was breathing, but it was ragged and unsteady. His body convulsed periodically and his tongue seemed too large for his open mouth. She heard Pea calling an ambulance behind her while she rolled him on his side in order to get him into the recovery position. As she did so, she noticed a small, crushed blue petal stuck to his neck. She frowned as the world seemed to swim around this delicate object so strangely out of place. She turned her head and looked up at the shelf to a white vase, which now stood empty.

CHAPTER NINETEEN

The next few hours passed in a blur. The police had arrived again en masse, with Corrigan at the forefront. He hardly spoke to Mary. Instead, they exchanged glances across the restaurant as people buzzed about looking for evidence of wrongdoing while he took statements at a table in the corner. When it was finally her turn, she sat in front of him with a blank expression, waiting to see what he would say first.

"I know what you're thinking," he said quietly, his dark brown eyes searching hers.

"I doubt it," Mary answered tersely.

"It's too much of a coincidence that just a day after Thomas Mosley's death, Spencer Harley collapses. You think they were both poisoned."

"Have you heard anything from the hospital?" Mary asked, not wanting to hear the answer.

"He's alive, but it's touch and go," Corrigan answered. "He'd be dead if you hadn't noticed the flower."

Mary felt a chill run through her. She had recognised the bright blue petal she had seen stuck to Spencer's neck as she had turned him over. She had seen it just that morning, though it felt so long ago now it could well have been months. The bright blue flower that had stood in the simple white vase on the shelf in the kitchen, which was now gone. She had informed the police, knowing that somehow it was relevant. Clearly, it had been.

"What is it?" she croaked, her throat dry. She reached down for the glass of water in front of her as Corrigan replied.

"Wolfsbane, or Monkshood. It's deadly poisonous despite its pretty looks. The leaves contain aconite, nasty stuff."

Mary took a deep breath and tried to arrange her thoughts. "How quickly does the poisoning take hold?"

"Very quickly," Corrigan answered. "You'd feel the effects within seconds depending on how you ingested it. Spencer..."

"It had to have been Ruth Faulkner," Mary said suddenly, cutting him off.

"Why do you say that?" he asked, sitting more upright in the hard-backed restaurant chair.

"She told us she was going home, the next thing we know she's screaming that something had happened to Spencer."

"She told us that she'd forgotten her phone." Corrigan shrugged.

"Maybe she did, maybe she didn't, but either way she was the one with Spencer, she had to have been the one that gave it to him." She paused, her own words confusing her. "How did she persuade him to eat something?"

Corrigan looked at her but said nothing.

"I mean, say she whips up something yummy and filled with poison. Surely it wouldn't be normal for her to just walk up to Spencer and shove a cake in his mouth."

"She didn't," Corrigan said.

"No, of course, she didn't, she would have had to tempt him, persuade him, but there wasn't time. She'd only been gone a few minutes after leaving us. Where would she have left the poisoned cake? Just in the kitchen, where anyone could find it? No, that would be crazy. Then again, maybe she is crazy..."

"Mary," Corrigan said in a firm voice. She jerked

her gaze up to him, her thoughts derailed. "No one baked a cake for the poison, they administered it directly."

Mary blinked. "What do you mean?"

"The petal you found on the victim's neck, we found more of them in his mouth. We think someone shoved the plant in his mouth."

Mary reeled with the image of this. Someone had physically forced a poisonous plant into Spencer's mouth? Who would do something like that? Something so up close and personal, something so brutal.

"I just can't believe we missed it the first time around," Corrigan said, shaking his head before pinching the bridge of his nose, eyes closed. "The bloody plant was right there in the kitchen the whole time, and we didn't even check it,"

"You weren't to know," Mary said. "They just looked like pretty flowers. You didn't even know that Thomas had been poisoned at the time."

"But you did," Corrigan said looking up at her. "You told me he had, and I didn't trust you enough. I'm sorry."

Mary felt a deep pang of guilt.

For most of her life, she had found that she'd never needed approval from anyone. She had largely done what she had wanted to do and pleased herself, not caring what anyone else thought of her. She realised now how angry she had been with Corrigan, how important it had seemed that she should be taken seriously, that she should be listened to. But why? She was an actress, not some crime-fighting superhero, and yet she had expected Corrigan to believe her. As he sat in front of her and apologised, she was realising how silly she had been.

"You had his food tested," she said. "What else could you have done at the time? Anyway, now we know, I assume you'll be looking to see if this is what killed Thomas?"

Corrigan nodded. "I've already called it in. Listen, Mary, whoever did this to Spencer must have been desperate. If Thomas was poisoned, which I now think he was," he added quickly, "then that was planned. It was cold and calculated. This was anything but."

Mary shook her head. "How on earth can you think of killing someone by stuffing flowers into their mouth?!"

"A crime of opportunity," Corrigan said. "Whoever did this to Spencer knew that the flowers were right there in the kitchen, and knew they were poisonous."

"So it's definitely the same person who killed Thomas," Mary said, thinking hard. She looked up at him, an apologetic smile on her face. "There's something I need to tell you." Corrigan's eyebrows rose. "Spencer asked me to come here, not because of the restaurant bash, but because he was being blackmailed."

"Blackmailed?!"

Mary nodded and watched as his eyes grew hard, his lips thinning.

"Why the hell didn't you tell me this before?" He said his voice like iron.

"He asked us not to! It turns out he already knew who it was, he just wanted me to find some evidence of it."

"Who did he think it was?" Corrigan said leaning forward, his voice was urgent.

"Roderick Sutton,"

Before she had even finished the name, Corrigan was up and stalking across the restaurant.

Mary stood and made her way across the room to where Dot and Pea were sat at a table.

"Where's he dashing off to?" Pea asked, peering at the commotion Corrigan was now causing amongst the three uniformed officers that were by the kitchen door.

"To question Roderick I'd imagine," Mary said as she sat heavily and put her head in her hands. "I just told him about Spencer being blackmailed."

"Oh, bloody hell," Pea muttered darkly. "How did he take it?"

"Unsurprisingly he was not happy that we hadn't told him earlier."

"Well, he's right," Dot added.

"Well, thank you Miss Obvious," Mary snapped. "Anyway, at least we've got to the bottom of how Spencer and Thomas were poisoned."

She filled them in on the blue flowers that had been in the kitchen and how they had been used. Pea's face, open like a book, as usual, moved through a range of shock and horror, while Dot's remained impassive, steely. Her eyes though seemed to flame with anger.

"Why would anyone do such a thing?" she said quietly when Mary had finished.

"I think we need to focus on Thomas," Mary said. "Joe was right when he said that poisoning Thomas had to be planned. Someone had thought it through carefully and managed to cover their tracks well. We still don't even know how he was poisoned!"

"Well, I doubt it was the same way Spencer was," Pea said, "Sort of thing a chap would mention at dinner, someone stuffing flowers in your mouth."

"No, he must have been given the poison some other way. What happened to Spencer was an act of panic. He must have found out something, maybe he knew who the killer was and they silenced him before he could talk?"

"I can't believe he was poisoned in the next room from where we were sat," Pea said sadly. "Poor Anna was here only a few minutes before."

"Anna!" Mary said suddenly, jumping up from her seat. "Someone needs to tell her!"

"We already have," Corrigan said as he made his way over to the table. "We called through to the restaurant where she was supposed to meet Spencer and have sent a uniform over to pick her up. Mary, can you come with me?" He gave her a small nod to follow him and turned away again. Mary looked at the other two nervously before following.

He led her across the lobby and through the door to the bar. Sat on a stool with a drink in hand was Roderick Sutton.

"If you'd like to take a seat, Miss Blake," Corrigan said.

Mary sat on a stool next to Roderick who was eyeing her suspiciously. She was feeling a rising sense of unease at the situation, not help by Corrigan being so formal with her.

"Now," the inspector said, standing between them and folding his arms, "Miss Blake here tells me that Spencer Harley was receiving blackmail threats."

"Blackmail?" Roderick said in surprise, he looked at Mary. "Blackmail about what?"

"I don't know, but I know that whoever was sending them wanted him to sell the hotel."

Roderick's expression changed from one of confusion to one of amusement.

"You can't think I was sending them?! That ridiculous!"

"Who else wanted Spencer to sell? Everyone else here would have lost their jobs if your plans to turn this place into flats had gone through."

Roderick's mouth opened and then closed again.

"Where have you been over the last few hours, Mr Sutton?" Corrigan asked.

"I... I was in my office."

"And where is that exactly?"

"I have a room here at the hotel, it's on the first floor. I can show you."

"And can anyone else vouch for your presence there?"

Roderick's eyes flashed between the two of them. "No. Look, this is crazy! You can't actually think I had anything to do with this. I don't know the first thing about poison!"

"If you could just wait here a moment," Corrigan

said to Roderick before gesturing to Mary to follow him again.

They stepped back out into the lobby as the Inspector closed the door behind him.

"I'm sorry I brought you into that, but I wanted to see his reaction when he realised Spencer had confided in you about the blackmail."

"And?" Mary asked.

"If I were a betting man, I'd say that was the first he'd heard of any blackmail, but I've seen too many good liars to go on that alone. What about you?"

"I thought the same as you, but I meant what I said. He's the one who has the motive for getting both Thomas and Spencer out of the way. It means he can sell this place and make his money."

Corrigan nodded, "Go back to the restaurant, I'm going to get his office searched and ask him a few more questions. I think it would be good if you were here when Anna Crosby turns up."

Mary nodded and was about to say sorry for not telling him about the blackmail letters, but he had already turned and headed back into the bar.

CHAPTER TWENTY

A s she turned back towards the restaurant, the main door to the street opened to her left and a uniformed officer stepped into the lobby and to one side. Anna Crosby entered arm in arm with Daisy White and moved towards her as the uniformed officer closed the door with him on the other side.

"Oh, Mary! Anna said, her eyes wide in horror. "Is it really true? Spencer's been poisoned?"

"I'm so sorry, but yes," Mary said as she took her hands in hers. "I thought you would be going straight to the hospital?"

"We tried," Daisy said at her side, "they won't let anyone see him at the moment."

Mary nodded, wondering if this was because Spencer was too ill, or if they were worried that his life was still in danger.

"I just don't understand how this could have happened," Anna said, tears rolling down her cheeks. "Why would someone want to hurt Spencer?"

"And Thomas," Mary said. She watched the shocked reaction of the two women before continuing.

"You mean," Daisy said in a small voice, "You think Thomas was poisoned as well? By the same person?"

There was something in her tone, something that sounded as though she was realising something.

"Daisy, do you know why someone would have wanted to hurt both Thomas and Spencer?"

Daisy's round, plain face creased with worry, her eyes darting left and right.

"If there's anything you can think of, no matter how insignificant," Mary continued.

"Daisy?" Anna said, looking at her strangely.

Daisy closed her eyes and took a deep breath. "Wait here," she said, before darting away and up the stairs.

Mary looked at Anna, who watched her go with the look of someone who was barely keeping a hold on reality. She looked ready to crumble. Mary put her arm around her shoulders.

"I'm sure Spencer's going to be fine, Anna," she

said, giving her a squeeze. "And we're going to get to the bottom of what's going on here."

Anna nodded before blowing her nose noisily.

Mary looked up to see Daisy hurrying down the stairs, in her hand a piece of paper.

"What is it?" Mary asked as she handed it to her.

"I...I think it's a blackmail letter," she said in a small, worried voice.

Mary opened it and looked at the sheet in front of her. It was printed in a standard font on normal A4 paper and looked like any short note you might find in an office. It read...

You won't get what you want Spencer,
it's pathetic. Sell the hotel now or
you'll be sorry.

"WHERE DID YOU FIND THIS?"

Daisy looked at the floor and bit her lip.

"Daisy, you have to tell me, was it in Spencer's room?"

She looked up and shook her head. "No, it was in Roderick's"

CHAPTER TWENTY-ONE

"And she just found it in his room?" Pea asked. "What was she doing in there?"

"Cleaning it," Mary answered. "One of the cleaning staff they hire in was off sick and so Daisy filled in. She was tidying some papers that he'd left on the side and saw the note."

"And she took it?" Dot asked, eyebrows raised.

"She was going to show it to Spencer, apparently. It had his name on it, she wanted to know if he was ok."

"So Roderick was the blackmailer," Pea said with a sigh. "Spencer was right all along."

"The silly old sod should have just been upfront with us from the beginning," Mary said with feeling.

She was altogether feeling annoyed about a number of things. Corrigan still seemed to be in a mood with her about not revealing the blackmail angle, even more so now that it appeared to be integral to the murder case. Roderick Sutton had been carted off to the police station for further questioning, and it was looking more and more likely that he would be charged with the murder of Thomas Mosley and the attempted murder of Spencer Harley. She hoped the word 'attempted' would stay in the second charge against him. As yet there was no change in Spencer's condition.

Although she should be happy at these recent developments, something was gnawing at her. They still didn't know how Thomas had been poisoned. How would Roderick have managed to gain access to his food? She had to admit, Roderick had a good motive for murdering Thomas. With him out of the way, the restaurant would be sure to fail and with it, the hotel. Forcing Spencer's hand to sell. In Mary's mind, it didn't fit with the blackmail. Why send Spencer blackmail letters if you had planned to murder Thomas? All the letters would do is leave a trail straight to you.

She leaned back in her chair and sipped at her coffee. The three of them were back in the restaurant, which was now empty save for one constable positioned in a chair by the kitchen door. He was reading a small pocket novel and seemed oblivious to them on the other side of the room. After giving their statements, Anna and Daisy had gone home, leaving the place with an almost abandoned air with Spencer in hospital and Roderick at the police station being interrogated.

"So he poisoned Thomas Mosley so that the restaurant would fail," Pea said thoughtfully. "He must have been bloody desperate for this deal to go through."

"Desperate enough to kill though?" Mary said shaking her head. "It doesn't seem that likely the place was going to survive in any case."

"Yes," Pea replied, "it's a shame he hadn't known Thomas was leaving beforehand. There was no need for him to do any of it in the end."

Mary sat up straight. "That's a bloody good point."

"I know that look," Dot said. "What are you thinking?"

"I think she was saying I've had yet another brilliant idea," Pea said causing Dot to elbow him in the ribs.

"What I mean is, imagine you had planned so meticulously to kill someone. You'd looked up how to get your hands on a plant that would do the job, you find some ingenious way of getting Thomas to eat it. Then, you have to watch him die in front of you."

She gave a slight shudder at the memory. "After all of that, you find out that he was leaving anyway, and that you didn't need to do any of it."

"Well yes, it must have been a bit of a choker alright," Pea said. "What's your point?"

"When I was speaking to Roderick, he told me that he'd only found out that Anna Crosby wasn't the real talent in the kitchen this morning when Edward Landry the hotel manager told him."

"He could have been lying," Dot said with narrowed eyes.

Mary shook her head. "You didn't see him, he wasn't the slightest bit bothered. He thought it was funny! Called it the hotel's 'little secret'. If he had really just found out, he'd gone to all that trouble, all that risk, and taken someone's life when he didn't need to, he wouldn't have reacted like that."

"So," Dot said slowly, "just because he was blackmailing Spencer to sell up, it doesn't mean he killed Thomas?"

"Not necessarily," Mary answered.

CHAPTER TWENTY-TWO

"I'm just saying that I don't think we should be going to someone's house like this when they've had a big shock," Dot said, her stout legs pumping alongside Mary's as she tried to keep up.

"Nonsense, she won't want to be alone at a time like this. She'll need company," Mary answered.

"From friends or family maybe, not from a bunch of strangers!"

"We're not strangers anymore, are we? Anyway, all we're doing is checking she's OK."

"Right," Dot said dubiously, "of course we are."

"Here it is," Mary said, stopping sharply, sending Pea clattering into the back of Dot who had followed suit. Mary watched as he fussed over her as he apologised and Dot shooed him away.

"You two are like some bad comedy act sometimes you know," she said, shaking her head.

"Quite the double act I'd say," Pea said, eyebrows waggling as he gave Dot a grin. She rolled her eyes at him and headed up the small path which led through the front garden, Pea in pursuit. Mary frowned at the pair. Something was definitely up between them, but it would have to wait.

She reached the red front door, paint peeling at its edges as Pea gave a rousing knock. The cottage was a small, but pretty affair. Roses trailed over a small roof which jutted out above the door, acting as a small porch, and its white walls looked thick and old.

The door opened and Ruth Faulkner appeared, looking around them in confusion.

"Oh, Ruth, we thought this was Anna's house?"

"Oh, it is! Ruth said, her warm smile returning as she stepped aside. Come in, come in! I had just popped round to see if Anna was OK," she said to Mary as the three of them passed her and moved into the house.

The inside continued the cottage feel of the exterior, with a low-slung beamed ceiling and a brick floor smoothed by time.

"Straight down the hall," Ruth called out, so Mary plunged in past small watercolours of various country landscapes until she emerged into a bright, wide and much more modern looking kitchen than could have been expected. A glass lantern roof hung over a dining table to the left while a sleek and ample kitchen sprawled to the right in what was clearly a significant extension to the older, original building.

"Oh, hello," Anna said as she looked up from a raft of papers that were spread on the dining table in front of her.

"Hi, we just wanted to check you were OK." Mary lied. In fact, Dot has been right to be suspicious of her motives for coming here.

She had at first intended to speak to Ruth Faulkner about the recipe book she intended to publish and had snuck behind the reception desk in the empty lobby at the hotel to do so. She had immediately found a sheet of hotel staff contact details pinned to the back of its raised front panel and dialled Ruth's mobile. After it had gone straight to voicemail twice, she had called the landline listed and had reached Ruth's mother who had told her she had gone to Anna's house.

"Would you like some tea?" Ruth said, moving towards the kitchen and clicking the kettle on before they could answer.

"Yes please," Mary said as she moved behind Anna and peered over her shoulder.

"I see you're working on the cookbook?" she said, spying that each printed page contained an image of some delicious looking meal or other as well as instructions printed below.

"Ruth thought it would take my mind off of Spencer for a while," Anna said feebly.

"Something positive to focus on until we can go and see him in hospital," Ruth called cheerfully over the rising noise of the kettle.

"And you're helping her with it?" Mary asked Anna.

"Ruth has very kindly offered to let me co-write it," Anna said with a sad chuckle that suggested this was more an act of charity than anything.

"Well," Mary replied, looking up at Ruth, "I would imagine having the name of a Michelin star chef on the cover would help sales significantly?"

Ruth paused for a moment before answering, her smile frozen in place. "Of course, it means we both benefit."

Mary looked at Dot and Pea, who had sat at the table opposite Anna and shared knowing looks between the three of them.

"These look very good," Dot said, taking one of the recipe sheets and squinting at it. "Did you two come up with them all?"

"They are all dishes we have cooked at the

restaurant," Ruth replied quickly as she rattled a spoon around in a mug. "Of course, they are mostly Thomas's recipes, but we are going to dedicate the book to him and I think it will be a fitting tribute." She turned back towards them with a steaming mug of tea in each hand and began to pass them out.

Mary stopped herself from asking when Ruth had begun writing the book after seeing the sad look in Anne's eyes. It had almost certainly been before Thomas had died, and so was hardly originally intended as a tribute. Anna though, looked as if she had enough on her plate without Mary opening her eyes to the manipulation by her friend Ruth. The question Mary wanted to know the answer to was, had Thomas known about the cookbook? And if he had known, when had he found out? Would he really have been OK with his colleague using his own recipes in order to make a book? One without his name on it. The more Mary thought about it, the more likely it seemed that Ruth had been assembling these recipes over time. Now that she was almost complete and looking to get it published, maybe Thomas had found out and threatened her? Maybe she decided that his recipes were such a cash cow that she thought it was worth killing for?

"How are you feeling?" Dot said to Anna as they all sat down.

"Oh, OK," she answered with a weak smile. "I just wish I could go and see him."

"I'm sure they'll let you in soon," Pea said, "even if it is with an armed guard!" The chuckle at his own joke faded as he saw the sharp look Dot threw him. "Sorry, bad taste," he mumbled before sipping at his tea.

"What about you Ruth?" Mary asked. "It must have been quite a shock finding him like that?"

"Oh," Ruth said with a shudder, "it was awful."

"I'm surprised the police let you go so soon."

There was a sudden chill in the room.

"Why wouldn't they?" Ruth answered. The slight smile was still present on her full lips, but it didn't reach her hazel eyes, which had turned hard and cold.

"Well, you discovered the body, I thought they would want to question you for longer."

"I gave a detailed statement," Ruth answered, "but I wasn't much help. When I realised I'd forgotten my purse, I came in the back way to the kitchen and found him there." She shrugged.

"And you didn't see anyone else?"

"No, obviously," she replied in a tetchy tone.

"It's just that, we know no one came through the kitchen door into the restaurant, so whoever did this to Spencer must have come in the back way."

"Mary," Anna said, her face pale." You're surely not suggesting that Ruth had something to do with this are you?!"

"I think she might be trying to," Ruth answered before Mary could respond.

"I think we all just want to get to the bottom of it," Pea said with a disarming grin.

"It sounds to me as though the police think they already have," Ruth replied.

"I can't believe Roderick would do such a thing," Anna said, shaking her head, her gaze distant.

"You'd be surprised what people will do for money," Mary answered, her eyes locked onto Ruth's.

CHAPTER TWENTY-THREE

"I'm sorry madam, you're not allowed down here, Inspector Corrigan's orders."

Mary glared at the young constable that had barred her way but turned back towards the road.

"Oh well," Pea said as she reached him and turned again to look back down the alleyway, "I'm sure the police will have done a thorough search of it all, so there won't be any clues still lying around down there."

"I wasn't looking for clues," Mary answered distractedly, "I just wanted to see if there were any hiding places."

The alley in front of them was nothing more than a gap that ran between two buildings, one of them being the hotel. The door to the kitchen was on the right-hand side, and the officious constable was standing before it as a silent sentry. Across from the door was a large wheelie bin, but nothing else seemed to be in the space from what they could see.

"What are you thinking?" Pea asked, looking at her with a furrowed brow.

"If no one passed us in the restaurant, whoever pushed those flowers into Spencer's mouth to poison him must have come through here."

"And how did Spencer get in?"

Mary's gaze jerked towards him sharply. "Bloody hell, Pea, good point. Spencer didn't pass us either, so he must have come through the back door with whoever attacked him."

"So we know he knew them, whoever it was."

"Well, we knew that anyway. Whoever murdered Thomas and attacked Spencer is definitely someone at the hotel. Only one of them could have brought the flowers in and left them in the kitchen ready to be used."

"Surely this is all just pointing to Roderick?" Pea shrugged.

"Or to Ruth," Mary answered.

"I just can't believe she could have done it," Pea said shaking his head.

"That's because she's young and beautiful," Mary replied in a mocking tone. "I think your sense of justice gets a little wobbly around those things.

Think about using your brain instead of your other parts. Ruth was writing a cookbook using Thomas's recipes. If they were as good as everyone says they were, then that book could have been a success. Especially with Anna Crosby's name on it as a Michelin starred chef."

"So you think that Thomas found out about the book and threatened to put a stop to it?" Pea mused.

"Exactly," Mary confirmed, "and then Ruth decided she didn't want to miss out on the payday and so got rid of him."

"But what about Spencer? She wouldn't have any reason to attack him?"

"He must have found out it was her somehow." Mary shrugged. "When he confronted her, she panicked and stuffed the flowers into his mouth. She had used them to poison Thomas and they were still in the kitchen so she must have just grabbed them in panic." She looked up at Dot who was pacing up and down on the pavement, her phone clutched to her ear. "Let's hope Dot's publishing contact can find out more about that book, that's what will give us a motive."

After leaving Anna Crosby's house, Dot had revealed that she had an old school friend who worked in the publishing industry, and might well be

able to find out more about the kind of deal Ruth
Faulkner had secured for her cookbook.

"I wonder what happened to the flowers?" Pea
said quietly.

Mary turned to him. "The flowers?"

"Well, I didn't see them in the kitchen when we
found Spencer, so where did they go?"

"The killer must have got rid of them somehow,"
Mary answered.

"But you think Ruth is the killer and she was the
one who found him," Pea countered. "She didn't
have the flowers on her, so where were they?"

Mary looked at the ground and kicked away a
stone with her dark leather boots. Pea was right.
Whoever had attacked Spencer had done so in a
panic. It had been a rash and desperate move that
couldn't possibly have been preplanned. So once
they'd committed the act, what then? Ruth Faulkner
had screamed as though she had just come across
Spencer, but that could have just been some added
theatrics to cover her own involvement. But the
flowers, what had she done with the flowers?

"How long do you think it was before Ruth left
us in the restaurant and then we heard her scream?"

"Ten, fifteen minutes, I'd say?"

"Then she must have attacked him not long after
she first left us. She must have met him in the kitchen

and he accused her of murdering Thomas and she panicked and used the flowers. Then she must have run out into this alley and got rid of the flowers somehow."

"The police must have found them then," Pea said. "You should get on the phone to your police chap and find out."

Mary was about to make it clear that Inspector Joe Corrigan was not 'her police chap', but she caught the look on his long, lean face. She recognised it from her childhood as the expression he wore when he was delighting in winding her up.

"I wouldn't count on the police to come up with useful," she snapped, directing her annoyance away from her brother, "they didn't even think Thomas had been murdered until someone else had died, despite me telling them."

"You're quite right," a voice came from behind them. Mary felt Pea turn beside her, but she was frozen to the spot. With a sinking feeling, she knew the voice was Corrigan's.

"We should have listened to you from the start," he continued.

She forced herself to turn, trying to arrange her features into something resembling calm indifference.

"Did you find the flowers?"

"The flowers?" Corrigan echoed.

"Yes, you know, the ones that killed Thomas and were used to attack Spencer?"

Corrigan folded his arms and sighed. Mary watched as Pea backed away quietly to her left before he turned and headed back towards the High Street.

"I know what flowers you're talking about," Corrigan replied softly. "And no, we haven't found them. I was just wondering why you are here and asking about them?"

"Well if you must know, I was trying to work out how Ruth Faulkner could have attacked Spencer, had time to get rid of the flowers, and then got back to start screaming as though she had just found him in the kitchen."

"And why would Miss Faulkner want to harm either Thomas Mosley or Spencer Harley?"

"I think I can answer that," Dot said as she moved alongside Mary with Pea in tow.

CHAPTER TWENTY-FOUR

"OK, Miss Tanner," Corrigan said, in a tone that suggested he was possibly getting tired of dealing with the three of them. "Let's hear it."

"Ruth Faulkner has negotiated a two-book deal with an advance of one hundred thousand pounds."

"Book deal? What book deal?" Corrigan's soft, round eyes suddenly sharpened.

"Something else you didn't know about?" Mary said quietly.

"It's a cookbook," Dot continued, shooting her a look, "Ruth was writing it using Thomas's recipes and was going to use Anna's name on it to make it sell."

Corrigan opened his mouth to say something and then seemed to think better of it. Instead, his eyes flicked to Mary and lingered on her long enough to cause a prickle of heat to rise up the back of her neck. Then he suddenly turned away and strode back towards the restaurant door.

"I don't want any of you leaving town," he called over his shoulder. "I suggest you all just try to enjoy your stay rather than being amateur sleuths."

Mary tried not to show how much this had annoyed her, but the slight smirk in Dot's expression as she turned to her let her know that she was blushing.

"So Ruth has a pretty lucrative book deal?" Mary said, deciding to change the subject. "That definitely gives her a motive."

Dot sighed and looked at her watch.

"Listen, Mary, I know that we've all been caught up in this, and no wonder, but I think it's time we all took a little break and forget about all this murder."

"We can't forget all about it!" Mary cried, her hands in the air. "Someone has died and someone else still might!"

"I'm not saying we forget about the whole thing, I'm just saying that I think we all need a break to calm down and relax a little. We're not going to get anywhere all wound up like this."

"She's right, Mary," Pea said, leaning in and putting one long arm around her. "I'm pulling big brother rank, we're all going to find a pub and sit in it until we find it hard to get out of our chairs."

Mary couldn't help but smile. She looked between the two of them. Her oldest friend. The woman, who now seemed to have always been there for her, a port in the storm of celebrity that had been her life for so long, but now would never be again. And Pea, her older brother, who was always trying to set her on the right path, always grounding her when she needed it. Which she had to admit, was a lot.

"OK," she said laughing, "Let's go."

CHAPTER TWENTY-FIVE

"You can't be serious?" Dot said in what Mary, even her own fuzzy state, noticed was a slightly slurred tone.

"Why not?" Pea replied. "I know this has all been a bit stressful, what with people being poisoned left right and centre, but let's be honest here. We've all been feeling more alive than we have done in years."

Mary found it hard to disagree with. After a solid pub meal of steak and ale pie, mashed potatoes and mixed vegetables, the conversation had wandered back to the topic they all knew they had been avoiding for the past few days... What were they going to do with their lives next?

Mary felt as though she had been wrestling with this question for a long time, though in reality, it had only been a few months. She was ashamed to admit that when she had first lost her role as Susan Law in the hit TV crime show Her Law, she had never considered that Dot's fate was tied up with hers. That the end of Mary's career meant, at the very least, uncertainty for Dot's. Not to mention that Pea had apparently been unhappy-looking after the family estate for years, and she hadn't even noticed.

Pea had now suggested something that she was almost afraid to consider. The idea was so ridiculous, so downright silly that it didn't even warrant discussion, and yet...

The thought of it had fired something deep within her. An excitement, thrill and terror that she hadn't experienced for years, if ever. She knew it wasn't just her. The animation in Pea's face, the sparkle in his eyes, and as for Dot. She was sitting in silence, arms folded, with a look of deep thought etched across her square face. Mary knew that look. It was the look she had when she loved the idea of something, but was mulling it over from all angles to check for flaws.

"You are saying," Mary said, sitting up in her seat. "That the three of us should set up a private detective agency?"

"Yes!" Pea cried, thumping the table to accentuate his enthusiasm and sloshing some of his beer as he did so. "I mean, we've got all this money now, what better way to use it than to set up a family business!"

"It's not quite your normal family business though is it?" Mary said before finishing her gin and tonic. She tried briefly to remember how many she'd had but gave up when she decided however many it was, it wasn't enough.

"We'd have no trouble getting work," Pea continued, ignoring her. "People would be queuing up to hire Susan Law."

"I'm not Susan Law!" Mary protested.

"Well, no, of course not, but it would still work like that. Dot can sort all the admin side of things, she's such a whizz at all that, and I can manage the finances and all that business."

"What do you think Dot?" Mary said, turning to her.

Dot looked up, unfolded her arms and took a long sip of her gin and tonic. "I think it would be fun."

Mary stared at her in amazement. Dot Tanner was many things. Practical, sensible, fiercely loyal, an absolute master of organisation, but frivolous and spontaneous... she was not. The idea that she would be willing to start a private detective agency because it would be fun seemed so alien that for a moment Mary was sure she had misheard.

"I beg your pardon?"

"I said," Dot repeated, more forcefully this time, "that I think it would be fun. The three of us aren't getting any younger and sometimes it's OK to do something silly."

Mary stared at her as though she had just grown an extra head. This wasn't the Dot Tanner she knew. This was something unnerving. A Dot Tanner who was OK with being silly. She looked to Pea for some kind of sympathy, but saw only that he was staring at her friend with a misty-eyed smile.

"Oh!" Mary said in shock, her head switching back and forth between the two of them. "How did I not see this before?!"

"See what?" Dot snapped, shooting her a look that seemed to bore into her brain and say with no uncertain circumstances that she should shut up.

"Oh," Mary said, hesitating under the ferocity of the gaze, "I was just going to say that, of course, setting up a private detective agency is the right move." She smiled at Dot. "I just can't believe I didn't notice it before."

Dot gave her a small nod back, a smile forming on her lips. "Then that's settled."

"Let's get another round in to celebrate!" Pea laughed as he rose from the table and headed off to the bar.

"You are a sly one, Dot Tanner," Mary said once he was out of earshot.

"Don't be ridiculous, Mary," Dot said, pulling herself up straight in her chair. "We're not giggling school girls. Pea and I just enjoy each other's company and I'd appreciate it if you didn't make too big a deal out of it until we've had a chance to see what it could be."

"Of course," Mary nodded with a serious expression before quietly singing under her breath, "Dot and Pea, sitting in a tree, K.I.S.S.I.N.G!"

Dot hit her on the arm, but Mary saw a coy smile on her lips as she did so.

CHAPTER TWENTY-SIX

Mary woke to the sound of her phone buzzing on the small bedside table. She groaned and rolled towards it, reaching out blindly and knocking it to the floor where it landed with a thump. She swore and tentatively opened her eyes, thanking the heavens that she'd had the foresight to close the curtains before she had crawled into bed. Even so, she winced at the thin bar of light that edged the thick curtain and filled the room with a dull glow.

She leaned over the bed and felt around on the thin carpet until she found her phone before lifting it in front of her. Her bleary eyes suddenly focused as she saw Corrigan's name on the screen. She tapped open the message and read.

If you can read this through the
  strength of the hangover you're
  almost certainly going to have
  this morning, you might want to
  know that we've arrested both
  Ruth Faulkner and Roderick
  Sutton for the murder of Thomas
  Mosley and the attempted murder
  of Spencer Harley. I guess you
  really can go home now.

MARY BLINKED AT THE MESSAGE, re-reading it twice before she pulled herself upright with only a minor groan. So it was over, they'd made their arrests. The only thing that surprised her was that they had arrested both Ruth and Roderick. Roderick had a good reason for the hotel to go under, and getting rid of Thomas Mosley would have been a more subtle way than bumping off his business partner, but somehow Spencer had been attacked as well. Then there was Ruth, she had had the opportunity, however small, to attack Spencer, but she would only have done that to cover up the murder of Thomas. So they must have been in it together somehow. There would be no other reason for both of them to be arrested.

There was no point sitting here wondering, she had to know. She dialled Corrigan and listened to it ring out before going to his answer machine. She hung up and threw her phone on to the bed as she marched towards the bathroom. Hangover or not, Corrigan wasn't dismissing her that easily.

It was only a further forty-five minutes, somewhat of a record for Mary after a heavy night, before she was moving down the corridor towards Dot's room. She rapped on the door, leaning on the wall for support as she did so due to a sudden, gin induced head rush. After a few moments, she heard Dot's muffled voice through the door.

"Who is it?"

"Who do you think it is?" Mary snapped irritably. "Let me in."

"Um, just a minute!"

Mary sighed and leaned her head back on the wall, closing her eyes. She opened them again quickly. Was it her imagination? Or was there a muffled conversation happening behind that door? She turned quickly and pressed her ear to the dark wood. Although muffled, she could distinctly hear two voices in hurried conversation through the other side of the wood. One of them was male. She rapped again on the door.

"Come on Dot, hurry up!" she cried, a smile spreading across her face. Dot Tanner was in there with a man! Oh, she was going to make her squirm about this one! After all the years of disapproval for Mary's own habits with the opposite sex, this was payback time.

"I'm coming!" Dot shouted back irritably. A few moments later, the door opened.

"Good morning," Mary said, arms folded and a wide smile on her lips. "And how are we today, Miss Tanner?"

"I'm fine thank you," Dot answered gruffly, pulling her light blue cardigan together at the front. Mary was enjoying the sight of her old friend immensely. Dot, normally so neatly and impeccably turned out, looked frazzled. Her hair was tousled rather than the usual neat bob. Her clothes were slightly askew, as though she'd thrown them on in a hurry, and most telling of all, her face was a bright crimson.

"Morning Mary," a male voice called from the back of the room. Dot moved aside and Mary saw Pea sat on a chair by the dressing table attempting to look nonchalant.

"Morning Pea," Mary said, eyebrows raised. "Sleep well did you?"

"Not bad, thank you," he answered before clearing his throat. "Anyway, I had just called on Dot here and we were about to come and knock for you."

"Right," Mary said slowly, looking between the two of them. She deliberately let the silence stretch out, enjoying the two of them shifting uncomfortably under her gaze until she decided to put them out of their misery. After all, underneath her amused and questioning expression, she was delighted. Who wouldn't be? Her best friend and her brother getting together would be just what both of them needed.

"Well," she said, clapping her hands together and breaking the spell of awkwardness, "things have progressed overnight and they've formally arrested both Ruth Faulkner and Roderick Sutton."

"Both of them?" Dot said in surprise.

"Yep, according to Corrigan."

"Oh! You've spoken to him then?" Pea said, rising from the chair and moving across to where they were still stood in the doorway.

"No, he left a message."

"And he... didn't say anything else?" Pea continued, glancing at Dot in a way that worried Mary in some indefinite way.

"No," she said slowly. "Why?"

Pea and Dot looked at each other with expressions that said 'oh dear' and sent her stomach into turmoil.

"What is it?!" she insisted.

"Last night," Dot began gently, "you don't remember when we got back?"

Mary frowned, casting her mind back to the walkthrough the chilled and rain-soaked streets to the hotel.

"Yes, why?"

"When we got back to the hotel?" Dot pressed.

Again Mary searched through the fog of her memory until suddenly she remembered Corrigan, there in the hotel lobby as they entered.

"I spoke to Corrigan?" she said weakly.

"Not spoke so much," Pea grinned, " more yelled at, swore at, threatened, that kind of thing."

"Oh, bloody hell!" Mary cried, sinking her face into her hands. "Let's go and find some coffee, you can tell me how bad it was on the way."

"Ok," laughed Pea, "but I warn you, it was bad!"

Mary sighed and trudged back towards her room to grab her coat, wishing that gin and tonic had never been invented.

CHAPTER TWENTY-SEVEN

The three of them were back into the now-familiar Tumbledown Café, sipping coffee in silence as Mary felt the eyes of the others boring into her. She continued staring at the coffee in front of her, trying to hold back the panicked waves of shame she was feeling. It was a feeling that was unfamiliar to her; she had always prided herself on being somewhat shameless. There had been all manner of drunken debauchery over the years, some of which had even turned up in the British gutter press in the form of lewd headlines and unflattering pictures. None of it had bothered her. It was all destined to be tomorrow's fish and chip wrappings. This though... She exhaled slowly.

"I called him an arrogant pillock?" she said quietly.

"Amongst other things," Pea replied with a chuckle. "I have to say, he took it rather well in the circumstances. He just told you to go and sleep it off."

Mary frowned and put her head in her hands. Last night she had given Inspector Joe Corrigan both barrels. Calling his handling of the case incompetent, questioning his ability as a policeman and also, apparently, insulting him.

"Oh, don't be such a drama queen," Dot said in her usual no-nonsense tone. "Inspector Corrigan is a big boy and I'm sure he's been called much worse in his time on the force."

Mary shot her an angry look before pulling her phone out.

"Well, I'm just going to call him and apologise and get it over with. That way I can find out what's going on with the case at the same time." She rose from her seat and headed towards the door. As her hand reached the cold metal door handle she paused, a small picture in a tatty frame to the right of the door catching her eye. In it was a young girl holding hands with a man who held up two dead rabbits proudly. Her eyes though, were fixed on the girl. There was something vaguely familiar about her. She shook the image from her mind and headed out onto the street, taking a sharp breath as the cold air hit her.

Corrigan answered on the second ring this time.

"And how are you feeling this morning?" he asked immediately.

"I'm fine, thank you," Mary answered, annoyed at his slightly mocking tone. "And how are you?"

"Oh, I'm fine. Just here, messing up the murder investigation, being crap at my job and just generally being a pillock."

Mary felt her cheeks flush and was glad she had stepped outside rather than let Pea and Dot witness this.

"Look," she said quickly, trying to deal with it like ripping a plaster off quickly, "I'd had too much to drink and maybe got a bit carried away, so I'm sorry. Now can you tell me why you've arrested two people overnight?"

She heard Corrigan take a deep breath in exasperation.

"It's over, Mary, we've got the people responsible. That's all you need to know."

"Why have you arrested both of them? Were they working together?"

Another sigh.

"It seems that way. It looks like the two of them were in a relationship. Both had reasons to get rid of Thomas Mosley and we've got evidence against both of them."

Mary frowned. She knew that one of the blackmail letters had been found in Roderick's room, but she didn't know of any evidence against Ruth other than circumstantial. Across the street, her eye caught on James Donovan, the barman from the hotel. He was waving down a taxi, which pulled to a sharp stop in front of him. He turned, looking behind him as Daisy White emerged from a doorway and climbed into the back of the car with him.

"What evidence have you got against Ruth?" Mary asked as her eyes followed the taxi pulling away.

"We found some of the flowers, the Monkshood, back at her house. We think they cooked it up between them, but they're not admitting it."

"How did she explain the flowers being there?"

"She said she'd never seen them before, that someone must have just dumped them over her garden wall."

"Over her garden wall?"

"We found them laying on her flowerbed. She probably just threw them there to hide them and planned to get rid of them later."

Something was itching at the back of Mary's mind, as though a small insect had crawled into her skull and was now looking for a place to burrow.

"Did Roderick admit to writing the blackmail letters?" she asked on autopilot.

"No, says he'd never seen the one that was found in his room before and didn't have a clue that Spencer Harley was being blackmailed at all. By the way, Spencer appears to be on the mend, they think he'll come round soon and as soon as he does we should get confirmation that Ruth Faulkner was the one that attacked him." There was a muffled voice down the line, someone telling Corrigan something. "Sorry, Mary, I need to go. Why don't you go back home? I'll let you know what happens. Speak later." The line went dead.

Mary walked back to the cafe in a daze, her mind elsewhere. As she stepped inside to the warm, humid air, she turned and looked at the small picture that was hung by the door.

"Oh bloody hell," she muttered as the weight of realisation hit her like a punch to the stomach.

CHAPTER TWENTY-EIGHT

"Sandra!" Mary called to the café owner who was buzzing between the tables.

"Yes, dear?" she said, coming over with a dirty plate in each hand.

"Do you know who this is in this photo?"

"Oh, that's Daisy White and her father, he's dead now, of course, poor chap. He was always out in Parchester Woods, knew the place like the back of his hand, and of course, he always kept the hotel well-stocked in rabbits!" She laughed and moved back towards the kitchen.

"Pea! Dot! Get over here!" Mary shouted as she pulled her phone from her pocket and dialled Corrigan. There was no answer. Whatever had pulled him away from their call was still clearly keeping him busy.

"We need a taxi right now!" she said as frantically searched for the number of the hospital on her phone.

"What's going on?" Dot asked as Pea headed outside to try to flag a taxi down.

"I think the police have arrested the wrong people. We need to get to the hospital right now."

There was a bang on the café door and through the glass Pea jerked his thumb over his shoulder at a taxi that was idling at the edge of the road.

CHAPTER TWENTY-NINE

It was forty minutes later when they pulled up outside the hospital. The drive had been a mixture of unanswered phone calls to Corrigan and Mary, explaining to the others her suspicions and why she thought Spencer might well be in danger.

The three of them ran up the steps and straight to the lifts to the left of the main entrance. They already knew where they were heading. Their call ahead to the hospital had been frustrating. The receptionist would give any details about visitors to Spencer Harley and certainly wasn't willing to get the uniformed officer stationed outside his room on the phone. She did agree to pass on a message to him, but who knew if she had or not? Mary only hoped they weren't too late.

The lift finally opened on the right floor and they

burst out of it at a run before realising they didn't
know whether to venture down the corridor to their
left or right.

"Which bloody way?!" Pea cried in frustration,
his long arms waving in the air hopelessly.

Before Mary or Dot could reply, a shout sounded
from the end of the corridor and a figure dashed
across from one side to another.

"That was James Donovan!" Dot said as a
uniformed police officer appeared in the opening,
shouting at Donovan to stop.

"Come on!" Mary shouted, dashing down the
corridor towards the running figures. Her mind was
racing with possibilities. What had happened? And
more worryingly, what was still to happen. She knew
that Spencer's room still had a uniformed officer on
the door, but if that officer was currently chasing
James Donovan, that meant Spencer might be alone.

As she reached the end of the corridor, instead of
following the running men to the left, she darted
right into a short corridor that ended in another door.
On the left were two sets of windows and doors
which clearly led into private rooms. She ran to the
first window and looked inside. The light in the room
was dim, but a figure stood in front of the only bed in
the room, obscuring its occupant.

"No!" Mary heard her voice echo in the corridor

without even realising she had shouted. She moved to the door and wrenched it open. The figure was facing her in the gloom, clearly alerted by her shout. It began advancing towards her but hesitated as Mary felt Pea and Dot move into the doorway alongside her. A small glint of light flashed at the figures side.

"You can't get past us all," Mary said, raising her chin defiantly, her fists clenched at her side. She was desperately trying not to think about what that glint of light could have been. Suddenly, she didn't have to.

The figure rushed back towards the bed as Mary reached out and flicked the light switch on the wall to her left. The bright ceiling lights flickered on to reveal the murderer holding a knife to the throat of Spencer Harley, whose pale face lay unconscious in the bed in front of them.

CHAPTER THIRTY

"Just think about this," Mary said softly, waving for Pea and Dot to retreat back to the corridor without taking her eyes off the young woman in front of her. She felt her friend and brother move away behind her and continued speaking. "There's no way this ends well from here, Daisy. All you can do is make sure that it doesn't get any worse."

Daisy White stared back at her, her round eyes shining, her breathing heavy.

"Spencer was always so kind to you," Mary pressed on, "I know you don't really want to hurt him."

"You don't know anything!" Daisy hissed, her voice raised in pitch through adrenaline. "What did Spencer do for me?! Nothing, that's what."

"He gave you a job, he looked out for you after your father died."

"Is that what he told you?!" Daisy laughed. "He wasn't looking out for me, he was looking out for himself! If he really wanted to help me, he would have just sold the bloody hotel and let me get what was owed to me!"

"Help me understand," Mary said calmly as she took a step forward. Daisy tensed and Mary paused again. "Your dad worked at that hotel for years and when it was sold, the Parsons made sure he had a share in the new venture. They didn't have to do that."

Daisy laughed and shook her head. "You'd never understand, you of all people!" She laughed again, but there was no humour to it. Her normally plain, rounded face was twisted in anger. "My dad put his life into that bloody place! And what did he get for it? Forced retirement and a small chunk of shares that were worthless as the place never made any money! Oh, and then, of course, there's the best bit, getting me a job at the same place that broke him so that I could suffer the same fate." She sighed and looked up at the ceiling. "Do you know what my dad did when he retired?"

"No," Mary answered. She had noticed that the

police officer had returned outside the window. Through the open shutters of the blinds she could see he was talking into the radio that was clipped to his chest. Dot and Pea were looking at her through one of the open slits and she shook her head at them and nodded towards the policeman. She saw Pea turn away and knew that he had understood. If anyone entered this room right now, Spencer Harley was likely to die.

"The day he retired, he came home and sat in his armchair and cried. He cried!" Daisy looked at Mary again now, tears of her own filling her wide eyes. "I lost my dad that day," she continued, her voice breaking. "A part of him, the part of him that made him who he was had died, and it was never coming back."

Mary waited a moment, seeing if Daisy was going to continue, but it was clear she was lost in her own memories now, her eyes unfocused and unseeing.

"And then he died," Mary said softly. "And you decided that you wanted what you thought your father should have had. You wanted a financial reward for all the years of blood and sweat he put into that hotel."

"Yes! Is that too much to ask for?! That someone might think, in-between making their fancy meals in the restaurant, or trying to make that dump a success, that maybe I didn't want to work there? That maybe I didn't want to follow my dad's footsteps and work my whole life only to have nothing at the end of it but an armchair and TV until I die?!"

"And when you realised Roderick Sutton had had an offer for the hotel you saw a chance of getting what you deserved?"

"Yes, is that so wrong? The hotel was never going to make any money, most of the rooms hadn't even been used for months!"

"And then Spencer brought Anna Crosby in."

"You think she had anything to do with it?!" Daisy laughed again. "She was bloody useless! Anyone with any sense could see that! But then.... Thomas." She seemed to sag as she stood, her shoulders rounding, her head bowing.

"Yes, then Thomas," Mary echoed. "He changed everything, didn't he? You knew the hotel was failing and that Spencer was going to have to sell sooner or later, but then Anna hired Thomas and everything changed. The restaurant business picked up, and it started to get a reputation. I guess the Michelin star was the final straw? You knew then that the restaurant just might keep the lagging hotel going forever."

"I wasn't going to wait for some reward that

would never come like Dad did. I decided to make things happen." Daisy was defiant now, as though daring Mary to say what she did was wrong, but with the knife still hovering near Spencer's throat she wasn't about to rile her any further. She needed to say whatever she could to protect Spencer.

"What happened to your father was very sad, but you can't punish Spencer for that. He cares for you Daisy, he told me so himself."

Daisy looked down at Spencer lying prone beside her, as though seeing him for the first time.

"He's going to get better Daisy," Mary continued, moving another step closer, "and when he does, I'm sure he'll understand. He'll explain to the police and may not even press charges."

"I didn't mean to hurt him," Daisy said, her voice barely audible. "He came into the kitchen and saw me with the Monkshood. He didn't even know what they were. He said they were pretty and tried to touch them, to smell them, and I pulled them away. Then he saw I was wearing rubber gloves. I saw it in his eyes then. He looked so sad. He knew."

There was the faint sound of a sigh and Spencer's head turned slightly towards them. Daisy inhaled sharply and jumped backwards, dropping the knife to the floor with a clatter. Spencer's eyes flickered and he let out a small groan before his eyes opened fully and focused on Daisy.

"Daisy," he cracked quietly.

Daisy flung herself forward, dropping to her knees as she took his hand and sobbed into his chest.

"I'm sorry, I'm so sorry."

CHAPTER THIRTY-ONE

"You, have got some explaining to do," Dot said as Mary Blake entered the bar of the Rudolph hotel later that day.

Mary was exhausted. She had given her statement to Inspector Joe Corrigan what felt like a hundred times, explaining exactly how she had known that it was Daisy White that had poisoned Thomas Mosley and attempted to do the same to Spencer Harley. She knew though that she wasn't done yet. Arranged in the bar was another audience who wanted to hear the story. Roderick Sutton and Ruth Faulkner, both now released without charge, were at the bar. Roderick behind it pouring drinks and Ruth sat at a bar stool the other side. A few feet away, Anna Crosby, Edward Landry and Dot and Pea were sat at a table.

"OK," Mary said, slumping into a chair at the table, "but someone better keep the gin and tonics coming."

"Not a problem!" Roderick called form behind the bar, "The woman who got Ruth and me out of that bloody police station can have whatever she wants."

Ruth picked up the tray from the bar that he had filled and walked it across to the table with Roderick grabbing two chairs for them. Mary took a gin and tonic from the tray and slugged at it thirstily before taking a deep breath and looking around at her audience.

"I just can't understand why Daisy would have done something like this," Edward Landry, his pinched face and fish lips pursed as though he'd tasted something sour.

"I think the death of her father affected her more than anyone realised," Mary answered. "She felt he'd given everything for the hotel and got nothing in return."

"He got a percentage of ownership!" Landry spluttered. "Anyone who truly loved the hospitality business would have been honoured at such a gift!"

"From what Daisy said, I think all he really wanted was a job," Mary said sadly.

"Enough of all this," Pea said leaning forward, "I

want to know how the bloody hell you realised it was her in the first place?!"

Mary gave a sad smile. "The more I've thought about it, the more I've realised that I should have seen it earlier. When we first arrived we heard that Daisy owned a stake in the hotel, but we never considered her as one of the people who would benefit from its sale. Everyone was telling us how much she loved the place, and how much it had meant to her father. It never even crossed my mind." She sighed and took another drink. "There was something else we missed about Daisy's father," she turned to Anna. "Do you remember telling me about how Daisy's father used to provide much of the food for the hotel through hunting and foraging in the woods behind the town?"

"Yes?" Anna answered, jumping slightly at being addressed, her hand rising to her mouth.

"I saw a picture in the café of a little girl and her father in the woods. I'd seen it before, but it was only when I saw it right after seeing Daisy across the street this morning that I realised it was her and that she accompanied her father on those trips through the woods." She looked around at the blank expressions and realised she had to connect the dots for them. "Someone had known that Monkshood grew locally, and more importantly, how dangerous it was."

"And Daisy had learned this for her father," Dot finished.

"Exactly. When she realised the restaurant was going to keep the hotel limping on, she knew she had to do something to stop it. Remember all those things that had gone wrong at the restaurant? The fridge breaking down? The electrical problems? That was all Daisy."

"And when none of it worked, she decided to stop Thomas," Ruth said, shaking her head.

"Yes. She realised that Thomas was..." she paused, glancing at Anna.

"Oh, it's OK," she said sitting upright, "Thomas was the talent of the restaurant."

"When she realised that Thomas was key to the restaurant's success," Mary continued, "she decided to get rid of him. I don't think it helped that Thomas probably ignored Daisy to a large extent. Am I right?" She looked around at the group.

"I guess so," Ruth shrugged. "Daisy is a quiet type, which wasn't exactly Thomas's cup of tea."

Mary nodded. "I don't know what made her think of it. Maybe she was just out walking one day, saw the Monkshood plant and decided on a whim.

However, it happened. What happened next was definitely planned."

"But how on earth did she poison him?!" Roderick asked, "We all ate the same food!"

"We did," Mary nodded, "I got the police to check everything straight away and they couldn't find anything. Obviously, they checked the kitchen thoroughly, but none of them thought to check the blue flowers that were standing in a vase on the shelf. To be fair, why would they?"

"But we know she didn't just shove the flowers into his face as she did with Spencer," Pea said, "we were with him most of the evening."

"Anna and I were with him all the time," Ruth said. "He definitely didn't eat anything that we didn't and no one went near him with the flowers."

"No," Mary answered, "because Daisy had put the trap in place days before. Thomas took the poison himself at the table, but it wasn't in the food." She paused, unable to resist letting the moment of drama roll out before her. "It was in the sugar he added to his coffee." There was an audible intake of breath from around the gathered audience.

"The sugar?" Anna said, "But anyone could have had that!"

"Not everyone," Mary corrected her, "on the night of the dinner, all the guests sat at one end of the table and the staff at the other. There was a sugar bowl at each end. Do any of the staff take sugar in their coffee?"

Anna Crosby's hand flew to her mouth. "Oh! Only Thomas!"

"Exactly," Mary said, "and she made sure the staff sat at that end because she showed us to our seats first."

"So she put the poison in the sugar cubes?" Pea asked.

"The police have taken them away for testing, but I'm pretty sure, yes."

"And what about Spencer?" Roderick asked.

"Daisy had been sending him the blackmail letters for weeks, she was hoping to scare him enough into selling the place."

"What I don't understand is what on earth anyone would blackmail him about?!" Roderick interrupted. "I told the police as much when they tried to pin it on me."

"It was Daisy who tried to pin it on you," Mary corrected. "She told us she'd found the note in your room, but really she'd just gone to fetch one she hadn't sent yet from the supply cupboard where she'd put it ready to go. As for what she was blackmailing him about." She smiled slightly. She had initially decided not to say anything about the blackmailing, but after a while, she had come to the conclusion that sometimes love needs a push. "She knew that Spencer was in love with you Anna," she said, turning towards her. Anna's normally pale face flushed a deep scarlet. "Daisy was threatening to expose your lack of experience in the kitchen and tell the local newspaper that you were only hired because of Spencer's feelings for you."

Anna shook her head and looked down at her hands, which were wringing in front of her. "I can't believe Daisy would do that."

"I think she thought Spencer would take the offer on the hotel and that would be it. When he didn't she started to spiral, becoming obsessed. That's when she decided to get Thomas out of the way."

"But she didn't even need to!" Ruth said angrily. "Thomas was leaving!"

"Yes, but Daisy didn't know that until afterwards. James told her and she was pretty upset and angry according to him. I'm guessing it was because she'd realised she might have got what she wanted anyway, without killing him. Spencer's been able to talk a bit since he came around, he's refusing to say what happened to him."

"What?!" Pea said, incredulous. "Why on earth would he do that?"

"I think he's still trying to protect Daisy," Mary shrugged.

"After she tried to kill him?!"

"Yes Pea," Mary sighed giving him a withering look, "he thinks of her as a daughter, he's not about to make things worse for her. Anyway, she pretty much told me what happened in any case. He came in and saw her trying to get rid of the poisonous flowers for the kitchen. She was wearing gloves and I think he realised what she'd done. She panicked and shoved the flowers into his mouth. He was lucky to survive." Mary lifted her glass and drained the last of the cool liquid before looking at Roderick. "I take it this is a free bar?"

CHAPTER THIRTY-TWO

"You seem to be developing a habit of solving my murder cases," Corrigan said, his deep brown eyes glinting with humour. Mary opened the boot of her car before turning to him.

"Well, someone has to," Mary replied, "and you don't seem to always be up to the task."

He raised an eyebrow at her, but she could see he was amused rather than annoyed. She threw her case into the back of the car and closed the boot. "In fact," she continued, turning to him with folded arms, "you might well see more of me from now on."

"Oh?"

"We've decided we're going to start our own private detective agency. We'll probably just take on small cases at first, but I think we could be good at it." She stared at him, daring him to laugh. There was no humour in his expression now, though. He looked thoughtful, serious.

"I think you're right. You'll be very good at it," he said slowly. "And I have to admit, I do like the part about seeing more of you."

Mary felt her face flush and cursed in her head.

"Well, I'm sure there'll be some favours I'll need from time to time. Looking up license plate numbers and that kind of thing."

"That's not exactly a service the police provides."

"Neither is solving murders apparently and as I've been helping you with that, I think it's the least you can do. And anyway, as you said, it gives you a good excuse to see me again."

Corrigan stepped towards her, his right hand reaching up and pushing a loose strand of hair behind her ear.

"Then I guess it's just something I'll have to get used to," he said, before leaning forward and kissing her.

MAILING LIST

G et FREE SHORT STORY **_A Rather Inconvenient Corpse_** by signing up to the mailing list at agbarnett.com

MORE FROM A.G. BARNETT

Brock & Poole Mysteries

An Occupied Grave

A Staged Death

When The Party Died

Murder in a Watched Room

The Mary Blake Mysteries

An Invitation to Murder

A Death at Dinner

Lightning Strikes Twice

Made in the USA
Las Vegas, NV
14 February 2021